RAZER'S RIDE

JAMIE BEGLEY

Razer's Ride

This book is a work of fiction. Names, characters, places, and
incidents either are products of the author's imagination or are
used fictitiously. Any resemblance to actual persons, living or
dead, events, or locales is entirely coincidental.

ISBN-13: 978-0615900308
ISBN-10: 0615900305

CHAPTER ONE

Beth pulled her little car into the vacant slot in front of the Buy-Low Market. Grabbing her list and oversized purse, she glanced at her watch, calculating that she had an hour to finish shopping for Mrs. Langley. The frail old woman had hired Beth to do what tasks she was not able to do for herself any longer. She was one of many clients that Beth had accumulated over the last five years. She had even hired a college student part-time to do the chores she was not physically capable of completing. Cleaning out garages, heavy lifting, and lawn work were often requests that she once would have had to turn down. Since she had been able to hire Blake, those jobs were contracted out to him while still being able make a small profit for herself.

It didn't take long for Beth to complete the list. Frowning at the sparse list of groceries, she worried about Mrs. Langley's decreasing appetite; she knew it wasn't her finances that were responsible for the small list. Beth handled most of her finances, having earned an accounting degree in college; the extra task of balancing Mrs. Langley's checkbook took little of her time. It had actually made her feel better about using the neglected skills that her monthly student loan payment reminded her she had worked hard to earn.

When she had graduated, she had literally stumbled into her business when her next-door neighbor became ill. Beth had volunteered to run errands for her until she recovered. From there, word of mouth had created a clientele that had provided a steady income, but left little free time. Her clients had started calling and asking for minor tasks to be completed that they were more than able to perform for themselves, often to fill the loneliness of their lives. Beth thought it was sad that they called her instead of their children, who often lived near, yet were unwilling to stop what they were doing to see to the parents who had raised them. Mailing her a check when she billed them provided a salve to their conscious.

Beth was putting the groceries into the trunk of her car when the sound of loud motors filled the late afternoon air. Tensing, she looked over her shoulder and saw the large group of motorcycles pulling into the parking lot. The tiny town of Treepoint had a motorcycle club that had taken over the peaceful town three years ago. Slamming her trunk lid down, Beth quickly opened her car door and got in, closing and locking the door. As she put her keys in the ignition, she watched as the bikers parked closely together.

The Last Riders were a motorcycle club whose actual home location was unknown to the majority of the townspeople. Many believed it to be nestled in the mountains on the border between Kentucky and Virginia. When they got in trouble, as they often did, the two bordering police departments often foisted the crimes onto the others precinct; therefore none of the crimes they were believed to have committed were ever prosecuted. They were growing larger and stronger in force with both bordering communities becoming frightened of the intimidating strangers that lived and played hard. Fortunately, they stayed to themselves and what trouble they got into stayed within their own cloistered group as well as the unlucky bars they picked for the night. The aftereffects would often leave the bar closed days for repairs. Usually one of the members would show up the next day with a wad of cash for the owner plus extra to silence them. It had become a regular source of income for the small business owners.

Beth watched from her car as the large group walked into the store. The men were all dressed in jeans and leather jackets with their emblem on the back. Everyone in the small lot gave them a wide berth, not wanting trouble. Seeing others panic as she had made Beth feel guilty, they had not acted any different than any other shopper going into the small store.

Several women were interspersed throughout the men. As one of the young women laughed, it drew Beth's attention. Mrs. Langley's granddaughter, Samantha, was walking with her hand through one of the larger men's belt. His arm was casually draped around her shoulders as he walked beside Samantha while talking to another biker, totally ignoring the scattering patrons. Sam was dressed as Beth had never seen her clothed before, and she had already developed a reputation before the bikers had made their presence known in town. She wore tight jeans that left her hips and stomach bare with a glinting belly ring that drew attention to her flat stomach along with a skimpy top, which left the globes of her breasts bare. Motorcycle boots completed the picture of a biker babe that Beth was sure would give her grandmother heart palpitations.

Sam was several years younger than her and, at nineteen, her body was lithe and firm, unlike Beth's own short, chunky frame. Beth was not overweight, but because of her small, five-foot stature, the weight seemed to pack on no matter what she ate. Thankfully, her job and exercise kept her from being a pudgy mess. When they entered the store, Beth carefully pulled out of the lot. She was worried for the young girl, though being well acquainted with Sam, she knew she would not appreciate any concern. Beth knew Mrs. Langley would be worried sick if she knew whom her granddaughter was hanging out with while Sam's father would be furious.

Vincent Bedford was president of the local bank. He was aloof and arrogant, saving his charming demeanor for the upper class of Treepoint society. Beth had talked to him when his mother-in-law had hired her when Mrs. Langley had surprised Beth by asking her to keep up with her finances; her son-in-law had agreed without a second thought. Vincent Bedford was not interested in what little his mother-in-law had, instead he kept busy kissing the ass of every rich and widowed woman in Treepoint. Beth turned onto the small lane that led to Mrs. Langley's house to drop off the few groceries she had requested. She was already planning ahead to the next assignment awaiting her attention; hopefully she would make it home before dark.

* * *

"Did you see that?" Razer asked the girl hanging on to his side.

"How could I miss it? She practically jumped into her car she was so scared. I bet she pissed herself."

Razer laughed and the others close by joined in, having also seen the luscious little blond scurry to her car.

Inside, they split up, gathering supplies for the coming week. Massive amounts of meat, chips and beer filled the three carts to overflowing.

"How are we going to get all this back to the house?" Sam questioned Razer as he pulled out the large denomination bills to pay the exorbitant checkout ticket.

"Maybe we should hire your granny's scared little mouse to deliver them," he joked.

"Don't joke. I bet she ran right to my grandmother's to tattle on me. Nosy bitch."

Train walked up behind her, running his hand over her ass and pulling her close to his jutting crotch. They ignored the gawking customers and sales clerk who were not used to such blatant sexual behavior in public.

"What's she gonna tell, Sam? That you're fucking one of us? What ya worried about? It's not the truth." He snickered, pulling her even closer.

"Don't worry, Sam, it wouldn't occur to that old woman that you're fucking them all," Evie muttered snidely as she pushed her to the side with one of the overloaded grocery carts and moved toward the sliding doors. "Put the groceries in my car," she directed the bikers, ignoring the angry glare directed her way from Samantha.

Sam turned bright red at the disrespect shown from the popular Evie. Feeling herself under scrutiny by the open mouthed clerk she snapped, "What are you staring at, bitch?"

"That's the way, Sam." Train eased his tight grip before dropping a kiss on her mouth, providing a show for the stunned people at the checkout. Angrily, Sam pulled herself away, stalking away from the audience that had formed in the busy store.

* * *

Beth let herself into Mrs. Langley's house, juggling the groceries carefully. The large home was more than the older woman could handle anymore. The formal furniture and decorative ornaments required constant dusting. The gourmet kitchen had long lost it's usefulness with no one to cook for but herself.

Quietly, she put them away before going in search of the older woman. She found her lying on her couch, taking a nap.

"Mrs. Langley?" Beth was about to turn away and leave her to her nap when she heard a tired voice respond.

"Beth?"

"Yes, it's me." Beth moved further into the room so that she could be seen without making the woman rise from her reclining position.

"I thought you might be Samantha. She was supposed

to stop by for a visit this week." Sadness shone from her pale blue eyes. Beth felt a lump in her throat, so many of her clients suffered from loneliness.

Feeling compelled to sit for several minutes, Beth listened to several anecdotes of Samantha as a child. As she listened, she found herself wishing to shake the girl in question for ignoring her grandmother, yet she knew it was useless to feel anger about something that was beyond her control. She was simply following her father's example; Sam's mother had been Mrs. Langley's daughter and had died in a car accident when Sam was fourteen. Waiting until the woman wound down, Beth interrupted her between stories.

"I am sorry. I didn't mean to disturb your nap. I just wanted to let you know I dropped the groceries off and put them away. Blake will be by this weekend to clean out your gutters and store away anything you no longer need."

"Thank you. I don't know what I would do without your help."

"I am sure your family would be more than happy to help."

"You think so?"

"I know so. Now don't nap too long or you'll be unable to sleep tonight. I'll see you Saturday. I'll lock the door on the way out."

Beth left her already dozing back off and was locking the heavy door when the loud sound of motorcycles again drew her attention. They were driving slowly down the speed-restricted lane, passing directly in front of the house Beth was leaving. Samantha was on the back of a large, black motorcycle, holding tightly to a different biker than she had walked into the store with. Beth felt her eyes on her as she passed and waved her hand in acknowledgment. Samantha turned her head in the other direction, blatantly ignoring the casual greeting.

Beth shrugged to herself, not upset at the snub. Samantha had never been friendly when their paths had crossed, often being downright *unfriendly*. She had tried not to let it bother her, but Beth couldn't understand why the girl disliked her so much.

The walk to her car seemed like a mile instead of the few feet it actually was. As she walked to her car, she glanced toward the bikes again as they passed. If it hadn't been so obvious, Beth would have gone back into the house until they were out of sight, but she was unwilling to make a fool of herself twice in the same day. She blew out a relieved breath as the last bike passed. That biker had been the one with his arm around Samantha at the store.

He looked her way as she walked towards the car. The breath she'd been releasing caught in her throat at his rugged beauty. His dark brown hair reached the collar of his leather jacket and was tied back with a skullcap. Sunglasses hid the color of his eyes, although they didn't diminish the strength of his gaze on her. Feeling scorched as their eyes met briefly, Beth saw his lips twist into a wicked grin as if he knew the feelings storming her body.

She moved more quickly towards her car, tearing her eyes away from the passing motorcycle and refused to turn when she heard him rev the bike's motor as if he was laughing at her.

Beth's fingers trembled as she fit her keys into the ignition. She didn't know why the bikers made her feel so uncomfortable. The only conclusion she had reached was that they incorporated every vice her father had warned against. Beth's parents had been born and raised in Treepoint. Her father had been the local Baptist preacher and her mother devoted to his work. Their expectations of her had been high and the community had kept their eyes on her, telling her father of each infraction that they felt, in their righteous way, was against his teachings. He had responded with hours of lectures and days of reproachful looks, making Beth feel often inadequate and bad.

Experiences that young girls often enjoyed, such as dances and boyfriends, became associated with feelings that brought displeasure to her father. Beth had two choices when it came to the demands her father's position in the community commanded; either to rebel or to submit. Beth was no fighter; she had caved to her parents' demands because of her sister. It had not been hard caring for Lily; while Beth felt smothered by her parent's restrictions, Lily had embraced them. The rules had provided safety and structure to the traumatized girl.

In showing an example of charity, her parents had adopted a little girl, Lily. Beth's mind shied away from the memories of her first meeting with the little girl, but she was truly thankful her parents had rescued the sister of her heart, if not blood. She was everything Beth was not; tall, slim, and radiantly beautiful, both inside and out. When you saw her, you could not take your eyes off her; it was as if you would miss something vitally important. To look at the pretty 19 year old, you would never know the hell her parents had dragged her from.

Lily had been tiny for her age, and her natural mother had skirted the law by never putting her in school. After adopting her, Beth's parents had told everyone she was actually two years younger so she would not be so delayed in her own age group. Beth loved her sister and, when her parents had been killed when on a charity mission, Beth had moved home to care for her until she finished high school. Lily was now a senior with graduation a few months away. She had more than caught up developmentally and physically, but they had decided to keep her age unknown. It had been their parents' decision; the school knew her true age. It was the community that was kept in the dark, believing her to be seventeen.

Beth pulled into her driveway, seeing the porch light on. Lily would be waiting for her to get home from work. The smell of food assailed her when she entered the cozy house.

"Hi, sis, you're late," Lily greeted and accused her at the same time.

"I know. I would have called, but I know how you are about me talking on the phone while driving." Beth removed her shoes and the band holding her hair tightly back from her face. Beth eased her sister's fears, understanding how traumatized she had been from their parents' unexpected deaths.

"All right," Lily instantly forgave her sister. "Let's eat; I am starving."

Beth laughed at her sister's slim figure. "You always are. I don't know why you can't gain weight the way you constantly eat. Must be good genes." Instantly, Beth regretted her words at the pain in her sister's eyes.

Quickly taking her arm and leading Lily back into the kitchen, she changed the subject. "What's for dinner?"

Laughing, Lily answered her question. "Your favorite; spaghetti." The girls set the table and within minutes were sitting down to enjoy the dinner Lily had prepared.

"So what have you planned for this weekend?"

"Nothing much." Lily shrugged, taking a slice of garlic bread. "Studying." Beth frowned at her short answer.

"Isn't prom a few weeks away?"

"Yes, but I am not going."

"Why? Doesn't Charles want to go?" Beth tried not to wince when she said his name. The young boy was nice, however he showed many of the same characteristics of their father. His self-righteousness often grated on Beth's nerves.

"No, and neither do I." Lily raised her hand when Beth would have protested. "You didn't go to your prom because Daddy wouldn't allow it. I just can't go when I know it wouldn't have been what he wanted, and Charles agrees."

Beth chose her words with care. "Lily, times have changed. The church is much more lenient than when Dad was pastor. I am not saying go out and get wild, just go out and have a good time. There can be a happy medium."

Lily just shook her head. "No, Beth. Please, I don't

want to go."

Beth started to argue with her sister over whether it was the prom she did not want to attend or the after-parties, which could get a little wild, when the phone interrupted her with the notes of "Into the Fire". Lily made a look of reproach at the music, but Beth ignored it. She loved music and enjoyed it, contrary to her father's teachings of it leading to sin and temptation. Beth wasn't about to let Lily guilt her into changing it into her own boring ring tone.

"Hello?"

"Beth. This is Loker James. I'm sorry to disturb your evening, but I have a situation on my hands I was hoping you could help me with."

"No problem, Mr. James. What can I help you with?"

Lily made a face at her as she helped herself to another serving of spaghetti.

"I just received a call from Mick at *Rosie's*. Dad is down there, drunk, and trying to get in fights with other customers. I was hoping you could send Blake down there to take him home for me. I'm in Washington in a meeting or I would do it myself."

"I can't send Blake, but I can take care of it for you." Mr. James's father, Ton, was a small man with a big name and an attitude to match. He was a sweet person when sober, but when he was drunk, he managed to convince himself that he was a badass. This often led to fights that he lost and sometimes trips to the emergency room to be patched up under his son's furious recriminations.

Loker James had hired Beth because his business had him out of town frequently and he wanted to maintain a watchful eye on his father.

"I don't know if that's the best option. Dad can be hard to handle when he's drunk." The aggravation in his tone came clearly through the phone. Beth grinned, she was well aware of just how cranky the man could be, having put him to bed many times over the last few months since she had been hired. This, however, was the first time she would have to enter *Rosie's* to retrieve him after a binge.

"I can handle Ton. Don't worry. Mick will help me get him in the car."

She was well acquainted with Mick. The bar's owner had attended her father's church and even continued when the new pastor had taken over at her father's death. Her father had wondered frequently to her mother if it was to repent for the sins he allowed to be committed within his establishment, or those he had committed himself.

Whenever the subject had been brought up to Mick, he would just change the subject to her father's sermon, which redirected the enthusiastic pastor from his determination of saving the man considered to be one of the biggest sinners in the congregation. His large donations soon stopped further attempts at saving his soul.

"If you're sure?" Doubt was now laced in his voice before Beth heard him sigh. "Call me when you have him back at home. If you run into any trouble, let me know immediately."

CHAPTER TWO

It didn't take Beth long to reach the bar on the outskirts of the town after leaving Lily to do the dishes, which she didn't feel at all guilty about. That was the one chore Beth despised, spending her childhood doing them after the many dinners her parents had felt compelled to have for members of their congregation had completely turned her off from wanting to do them.

Beth swallowed hard when she pulled in and saw the parking lot of *Rosie's* packed. Friday was a busy night for the bar, but the vast majority of spaces were filled with motorcycles. A sinking feeling hit her stomach. Before she could change her mind and call Loker James back to tell him that she couldn't rescue his father, Beth walked quickly to the entrance. As she neared the doorway, a movement to the side of the business drew her attention.

A male was leaning against the side of the building, the darkened wall providing support as a woman with a frilly black skirt was on her knees before him. Her bobbing head showed exactly what sexual act she was performing on the male with his cock buried in her mouth. When Beth was able to lift her shocked eyes from the thrusting hips and large member being shoved into the woman's eager mouth, she recognized the man from earlier today as the one who had seen her scurrying to her car. Even now, Beth had to stop herself from running back to the safety of the waiting vehicle when he lifted his gaze and saw Beth staring at them in shocked surprise.

He did not slow down, instead the hand in the woman's hair tightened as he pulled her closer onto him. He momentarily broke eye contact with Beth to watch his length disappear into the woman's obviously experienced mouth. Her black tube top was down around her waist and his fingers were tugging on the woman's breast in his hand. Beth saw his fingers twist her nipple and the woman began to squirm as her head bobbed faster until Beth could tell from his lustful groan, as well as the woman's gasps, that he was coming in her mouth.

When a slamming door jarred her back to reality she walked jerkily forward, practically running into the bar. Beth despised herself for watching the couple, but she had been frozen in place, unable to move with his eyes pinning her there.

It took several seconds for her eyes to adjust to the dimness of the bar. Looking around, she saw Ton sitting at the bar and it seemed she had arrived just in time. He was currently being held by the throat by another biker she had seen with Samantha, who was now sitting on the lap of a heavily tattooed biker, earlier that day.

Guessing fidelity did not exist among the group, Beth motioned to Mick who had not taken his eyes off her since she had entered the bar. Carefully walking up behind Ton, who couldn't see her approach due to the biker now holding him dangling in the air, Beth reached out a hand and tugged at the arm determined to strangle the life out of her client.

"Excuse me, could you please let him go?" The unbelievably scary face that turned to her forced an unintended squeak past her trembling lips. Beth knew she was a self-confessed coward and wisely would have never in a million years attempted to confront the huge being in front of her in usual circumstances. This was definitely far from usual. She was being forced into the confrontation for her client's well-being and, of course, the huge amount she was planning on charging Loker James.

Swallowing the huge lump of fear lodged in her throat, she reached out and tugged his hand away from a purple Ton.

Released, Ton grabbed the bar, hanging on as he dragged air into his oxygen deprived lungs. His gasps for air drawing everyone's attention as they waited to see if the old man would have a heart attack or recover.

"What the fuck?" When the huge biker moved forward to grab Ton again, Beth moved, placing herself in front of Ton and thereby, blocking his access.

"I apologize for anything and everything he has done. I am here to pick him up. If you would give me a minute, I will get him out of your hair." Belatedly, Beth noticed the scary biker dude had no hair. "I mean—" hastily Beth spoke once again. "I know he can be a little irritating when he has been drinking, and I won't let him bother you further."

The silence in the bar allowed Beth to hear her thundering heartbeat.

"He called me a pussy. I am going to beat the shit out of him then you can take him wherever the fuck you want to." Again, he reached out to grab Ton, shoving her out of his way.

As Beth grabbed a stool to regain her balance, she heard a harsh voice directed at the meathead. "Back off, Knox. Let him go. You can settle the score later."

Beth turned to see the man from outside shoving the huge man's back. The woman who had been giving him the blowjob followed meekly behind him before giving Beth a wink and going behind the bar where she immediately began filling glasses with foaming beer.

Beth felt herself turning red, unable to meet his eyes.

She was angry that she continued to make a fool of herself in front of this particular biker.

The man called Knox looked as if he was going to argue before grinning at her, raising his voice so that Ton could hear him. "Count yourself lucky, old man, that tonight this sweet looking bitch showed up, but I will be dealing with you later. I am tired of your mouth spouting off what you're too old to back up."

Ton, with his oxygen restored, if not his sanity, responded unwisely, "You see what I mean, Beth. He's a pussy."

Beth screamed as Knox lunged for the unrepentant Ton, knocking her sideways as the bikers moved to hold Knox back.

Beth found herself grabbed and held until she was able to regain her balance. Looking up, she saw eyes staring down on her that forced feelings from her body that had been repressed for years. She pulled away from the hard body supporting her, uncomfortable with the memory of his sexual encounter with the waitress just a few minutes ago. A red faced Beth turned to see the heavily tattooed biker holding back a struggling Ton, while four others held back a furious Knox.

"This is my bar, and I don't care much what goes down in here as long as your money is green," Mick bellowed, drawing everyone's attention. "But I am going to have to tell you to leave Ton alone. I am friends with Loker, and I am telling you he will make amends for his father."

Beth was surprised at the reaction that drew from the bikers. Even the furious Knox hesitated. Taking advantage, she moved to take Ton's arm, determined to get out of the bar while Mick held their attention; however, Ton wasn't having it.

The obnoxious man jerked away from her touch. "I ain't going nowhere till I get another drink."

"Please, Ton, let's just go. Mr. James wants me to take you home. He's waiting for my call."

"Then he can wait ten more minutes because I am getting my drink." The belligerent man stomped to a nearby table and yelled at Mick, "I'll have another whiskey."

Mick just stared at him before turning to the woman behind the bar. "Jenna, get him a whiskey." Looking at the bikers in warning, he went back to the bar and began serving drinks. "Round of beers on the house." Mick's words had the bikers moving to the bar.

Beth didn't miss the threatening glare Knox threw Ton before reaching for his beer and leaning against the bar, not taking his eyes off the drunken man.

Beth, not knowing exactly what to do in this ludicrous position, took a chair at the table next to Ton. When the waitress put the whiskey in front him, she didn't raise her eyes. She already had seen too much of the woman.

"Can I get you anything?"

"No thanks."

"Suit yourself." Beth raised her eyes to see the amusement in Jenna's expression. Beth became aware then that the woman knew that Beth had seen her sexual act outside and could not care less. She watched as she served drinks to the men in the bar, flirting with several of the bikers.

Beth surreptitiously looked at the biker Jenna had given the blowjob and saw no jealously. Instead, he was staring at her. Her face reddened with embarrassment when he took a seat at the small table next to her. His thigh brushing hers before Beth hastily moved it away.

"You know you've placed Loker in a bad position, Ton," the biker said.

"It won't be the first time and definitely won't be the last, Razer." Ton raised his glass unconcerned. "Besides, Loker can take care of himself."

Razer lifted his beer to his lips. Beth couldn't help noticing how sensual they looked as he took a drink. He was a good-looking man and, from his attitude, he was well aware of his attraction to the opposite sex. She could tell that he was not surprised to find Beth staring at him.

"After he finishes his drink, you need to get him out of here. If he mouths off to Knox again, nobody will stop him." He cast a warning look to Ton while talking to Beth.

"I'm going." Ton stood up shakily from the table. "Not because I am scared of that."

"Ton don't," Beth pleaded.

Not to be stopped, Ton continued, "But I have to get Beth home. She doesn't belong in this dump."

Beth wanted to yell at the man herself for insulting Mick's business. He had saved the ornery man's ungrateful butt. Seeing Mick stiffen behind the bar, Beth knew Loker would be making amends, and not only to the bikers.

Beth rose from the table and moved to follow Ton towards the door. Taking her hand, Razer spoke directly to her for the first time. "Why don't you drop off Ton and come back. Have a drink with me."

Beth's mouth dropped at the arrogance of the man. He was definitely used to women being available to him.

"I don't think so. Thanks anyway." The polite Christian girl inside her refused, while the wild woman she used to dream about begged for release. Jerking her hand from his, she hastily followed Ton outside with Razer's laughter following her. He had seen her indecision.

* * *

"What the fuck was that about?" Samantha said, walking up to the table.

Razer knew she had overheard him. "It's none of your business." He gave her a hard look, letting her know that he wouldn't take her shit.

"Come on, Razer. I'm horny. Let's head home."

"What's the matter? Shade not in the mood?"

"You know I can handle you both." Leaning against his back, she rubbed her breasts against him. Her hand trailed down his chest until her hand covered his crotch, squeezing him through his jeans. His cock hardened against her experienced fingers.

Pulling her to the side, he jerked her down for a rough kiss. "Get Shade and meet me outside. I'll pay the bill and be there in a minute."

"Why pay Mick? He said it's on the house? If you want to blow your cash, give it to me." Razer became ice cold. "We always pay our way. Mick isn't responsible for Ton. Quit being a greedy bitch and go outside to wait, or I'll ask Jenna if she wants to play. Makes no difference to me," he ordered.

Sam bit back the sharp retort she wanted to make, but knew she would make Razer angry with her and she wanted him too badly for that. She had seen the interest in his eyes when he sat down next to the goody-two-shoes, Sunday school teacher. She would've sworn before that he didn't stand a chance in hell in getting into those panties, yet Sam had seen the slight hesitation in Beth when he had asked her for a drink. Determined to give him a night he would never forget, she went to get Shade and wait outside.

* * *

"Get up sleepyhead." Beth burrowed further under her pillows at her sister's demand.

"Go away." She felt like she had just closed her eyes.

It had taken her over an hour to get Ton taken care of and then she'd had to place the call to explain everything to Loker, who had been surprisingly calm at her description of the events. He had always been a mystery to her. In his late thirties, he was not a handsome man. He was known to be harsh and unfriendly around town, however it didn't matter because he was a well-known businessman who had made Treepoint his home when his father had retired here after retiring from the Army.

He had hired Beth when his business trips began lasting longer than several days. Ton was a well-known rebel rouser around town when he was drunk, but he also had several medical conditions that needed careful monitoring. Beth was amazed he had managed to make a career out of the Army with his behavior. Lily bounced up and down on her bed, pulling her away from her thoughts.

"Let's go swimming," Lily suggested

With her weekdays usually full, Beth kept her weekends free to spend with Lily. Her departure in two months for college was looming and Beth wanted to spend what time she could with her before she left. Sadness clutched at her chest at the knowledge things were about to change. They had such a close relationship and Beth didn't want them to grow apart.

"Okay." Laughing, they scurried into their suits, covering them with shorts and t-shirts. Beth enjoyed her relaxed attire, instead of her regular professional dress-code, when about town dealing with her clients.

After eating a quick breakfast and packing a light lunch, they got in Beth's car to head to the small lake nestled in the base of the surrounding mountains. Ordinarily it wasn't busy this time of the year, but Beth and Lily had discovered a small nook with a tiny beach that no one ever went to that allowed them even more privacy. They frolicked and played for over an hour before getting out and lazily eating their lunch.

"Ready to go back in the water?" Lily asked.

"You're supposed to wait twenty minutes or you'll get cramps," Beth replied, stretching out and relaxing on the soft blanket they kept in the car for such occasions. Both sisters were avid swimmers and the cold water was never a deterrent.

"That's an old wives' tale."

"I don't think so. Sounds true to me."

"Lazy butt, you just don't want to get up."

"I'm not seventeen with boundless energy. I am old."

"You're twenty-four; that's not old. Besides, I'm nineteen remember?"

"It feels old, and you act seventeen."

"You're only tired because you got in so late last

night."

"How do you know what time I got back? Your light was off when I got home," Beth questioned.

"I wasn't asleep. I can't sleep until I know your home," Lily confessed.

"It won't happen again. I am sorry," Beth apologized.

Lily shrugged. "It's not your fault. I need to get used to being on my own unless I go to the community college in the fall to stay closer." Lily watched for her sister's reaction.

Beth shook her head negatively. "I told you it would be good for you to go to a college further away from home. There is a whole world out there for you to discover. Give it a couple of semesters. If you're truly unhappy, then come home. You know if you want to be a social worker, then you need the advantage of a broad spectrum of experiences."

"But…"

"Give it a try." Beth smiled.

"All right, but if I'm unhappy, I am coming home."

Laughing, Beth jumped up and grabbed her hand "Let's go swimming."

"What about waiting?"

"Let's live dangerously." They giggled as they ran into the cool water, taking turns dunking each other and simply spending time together.

After some time, Beth was finally frustrated at being unable to catch her slippery as a seal sister and headed back to their blanket.

"I'll pack up if you want to swim a little longer," she said over her shoulder.

"Cool." Lily lazily floated on her back as she waved her sister away.

Smiling, Beth was kneeling on the blanket putting away the remains of their lunch when she heard the loud motors coming their way. She began praying they would pass by, however her prayers remained unanswered as the large group of bikers rode into the small nook.

Beth remained frozen as she watched them get off their bikes and then pulled beer and towels out of the side bags attached to the motorcycles. Beth recognized Razer, Knox and Samantha, who had ridden in with five other women on the back of the bikes, though the rest of the group of twelve were unfamiliar to her.

Beth recognized the biker Sam had ridden behind from the bar last night, his heavily tattooed body made him impossible to forget. He had dark hair like Razer's, but cut shorter, he was also leaner with an air of menace that clung like a glove. His eyes were covered with sunglasses, yet Beth could sense him taking in the position of both herself and Lily.

Her eyes turned to Lily who had been swimming back toward the shore when the motorcycles had turned into their isolated spot. Beth, like her sister, had frozen in place; Lily's beautiful face showing a mirror of her terror.

With her eyes on her sister, Beth felt someone approaching her as she sat frozen on the blanket.

"Mind if we join you?"

"Not at all, but as you can see, we're about to leave." Beth kept her voice even to avoid frightening her sister. Lily was terrified enough.

Beth didn't think the group would accost them; word would have gotten around town if they had a reputation of bothering women. In fact, the bikers really didn't have to worry about hounding women; the shortage of available males in the community provided them with plenty of women to choose from.

Razer's direct gaze pinned her to the spot. "We can't tempt you to stay?"

"No. We've been here awhile and the sun is getting to us." Razer studied the woman sitting on the blanket. Her pale blond hair was beginning to dry. Parted down the middle, it framed her face before curling underneath. The thick mass was long and silky. Her fair skin was a faint red, showing that the sun was beginning to take its toll. The pale curves of her full breasts were barely hidden by the light blue, one-piece suit she was wearing.

"I bet that isn't all that's getting to you," Sam said snidely, brushing up next to Razer. Her sharp gaze was pointed at Beth's swimsuit top. Beth blushed, aware the girl saw her pointed nipples through her still damp suit.

"Ignore her. She's a bitch, but I'm sure you know that since you've lived around her longer than I have. Hi, I'm Evie."

"Hi." Beth acknowledged the pretty brunette while continuing not to take her eyes off of Lily. Standing, Beth pulled on her shorts self-consciously and was about to reach for her t-shirt when she noticed that Razer already had bent down to get it. He stood, holding it in his hand, and, when she reached to take it, he wouldn't let it go at her sharp tug.

"Everything all right?" He was staring at the still frozen Lily.

"Yes, everything is fine." Hastily pulling her shirt from his grasp, she put it on, bending to pick up the blanket.

"She okay?" Evie looked in concern toward Lily, who was beginning to tremble. For the first time, Beth took her eyes off her sister to look at the men. Their expressions were hard to hide, however they weren't what Beth thought she would find. They were all concerned. At that realization, Beth's worry about their appearance disappeared. Lily was wearing a tiny pink bikini that showed the maturity of her figure, so for them to see the fear she was exhibiting and not salivating at her lithe body gave Beth peace of mind as to their intentions.

"Hey, we can leave," Razer offered.

"No… No, it's fine." With the blanket in her hands, Beth walked slowly towards her sister. "Lily, I finished packing everything. Are you ready to leave?"

Lily shied away from her, back into the water. Her hands were now crossed to cover her breasts, which only pushed the firm flesh higher. Beth stopped, remembering how this had happened once before when an intoxicated parishioner had shown up at her parents' house, carrying a liquor bottle. It had taken Beth several hours to get Lily out of her daze. Beth didn't have to guess the nightmares she was reliving. She knew. It was the same reason that Lily was determined to be a social worker; the dedication she had was the only thing that could lure her away from the safety she had found in the mountains.

"Lily, please. They won't hurt you. They haven't even started drinking yet." Which Beth hoped was true. "You have nothing to be afraid of. Have I ever let any harm come to you?"

A small moan passed Lily's trembling lips as she took a hesitant step toward Beth. "That's it, sweetheart," Beth praised.

"For Heaven's sake, leave bitches. No one wants you here anyway."

Out of the corner of her eye, Beth noticed Razer motion for Evie to get Sam quiet.

"Why do I have to shut the fuck up? That skinny slut thinks she's better than us—" Beth heard a sharp yelp as Evie's hand smacked Sam's mouth, effectively cutting the girl's sentence off.

"I told you to shut up." Finding herself surrounded by the other women, Sam finally kept her mouth closed.

"Beth…" Lily's broken voice tore at Beth's heart.

"Come on, sweetheart; a few more steps." Beth waited patiently on shore, aware that the bikers stood immobile. Finally, Lily walked within reach and Beth wrapped the blanket around her shivering form. Tugging her from the water required every ounce of strength she possessed. As they drew closer, the men in the group pulled back, giving Lily the space she needed. Finally, Beth was able to maneuver her into the car. Hastily she moved towards the driver's door where Razer had stopped to hand her the towel and basket she had left behind.

23

"Thanks," she said.

"She going to be okay?"

"Yes, she'll be fine when I get her home," Beth tried to explain while remaining tactful. "It's not you guys, it's the liquor."

Razer smiled, showing that he knew she was lying. "I think a rowdy gang of bikers probably didn't help the situation." When Beth would have denied it, he forestalled her. "It's cool. No offense taken. We scare everyone in this small town. Two lone women in an isolated spot, you would be crazy to have no concerns when we invaded your space."

Beth smiled at him naturally for the first time, blushing as he grinned back.

Not wanting to keep Lily waiting longer, Beth got inside the car. She gave her sister a concerned look as she pointed the car towards home. When they arrived, she made a hot bath for Lily and a light dinner of chicken salad. They sat quietly munching without talking. Lily had demons in her past that certain events triggered and Beth had learned long ago that it was best to let Lily battle it out herself. Even without Beth's aid, she would usually realize it had been an over reaction and then strive harder next time to keep better control of her fears.

Later in the night, though, screams startled her awake. Running into Lily's room, she found her curled into a ball in the corner. Beth sat down next to the crying girl, pulling her into her arms to offer what comfort she could while smoothing down her dark curls. Beth rocked her sister until she fell asleep. Gently disengaging herself, she went to the bed where she removed the comforter and pillows. Placing the comforter on the floor, she maneuvered her sleeping sister until she lay prone on the thick material. Beth lay down next to her, raising her head and putting the pillow beneath it.

They slept curled together as they had done many nights when they were children. Beth felt tears slide from her eyes at the thought of the pain Lily had endured as a child; she had survived only to have the brutal memories there, waiting for a chance to attack. Beth whispered into the darkened bedroom the same prayer she had uttered every night since Lily had become her sister. That she find peace from her nightmare and someone strong enough to give it to her.

CHAPTER THREE

Beth saw that Sunday morning had turned out to be a pretty one as she woke a groggy Lily to get ready for church. They had never missed a morning service and, even after their difficult night, it never occurred to either of them to not attend.

The service was positive and left each girl in a lighter mood, unlike the ones her father used to give. Afterward, they walked to the local diner, which was just across the street. Lily's friends joined them and they ended up at a large table. Her friends were boisterous, as kids their age usually were, but Lily didn't mind joining in with her own wicked sense of humor. Beth sat at the opposite end of the table, contently sipping her coffee while watching the shadows in her sister's eyes disappear into their lovely violet depths. The restaurant around them was packed with people standing around, waiting for a table to empty.

"Pastor Dean!" Lily waved at their Pastor when he walked into the restaurant. The good-looking Pastor Dean had received many invitations to lunch after the services, but he always declined. Eligible, young and extremely handsome with mahogany hair, the women in the church were always vying for his attention. She was therefore a little surprised when he excused himself from the parishioner he had been talking to and made his way to their table. Beth watched as he greeted Lily and her friends, the respect they had for the man was obvious. It was no wonder that they respected him; he was a very good pastor who made time for his parishioners, including the young ones, when he had begun earning their trust.

He had taken over for her father two years ago and at first had met resistance from within the church. He was more lenient where her father had been hell and brimstone. Beth didn't resent the change, though, in fact she was happy that the younger crowd wouldn't be taught in such a stifling atmosphere.

"Would you like to join us?" Beth asked when she could get a word in.

Pastor Dean laughed. "I would." Pulling a chair out next to Beth, he sat down. "It'll give me a break from the more stodgy parishioners."

"Now, pastor, we don't want to deprive your flock of your company." Beth laughed.

"Please deprive away." Dean ordered his breakfast from a passing waitress. "Unless you need my advice on your everlasting soul."

Beth shuddered. "No, I'm good."

Dean laughed again, quickly drawn into a conversation with the others at the table. The youth group was planning a weekend trip to donate their services to rebuild a church that had been destroyed by a tornado, and the kids were talking animatedly about it. It was an enjoyable lunch with at times serious topics.

As the lunch crowd in the restaurant began to thing out, Beth noticed the table in the corner against the back wall. Razer and two of his buddies sat watching her table.

"Beth!" Lily drew her attention. "We're going to the movies and then to Charles's for dinner. We need to finish a PowerPoint presentation for class tomorrow."

"Okay, take the car." Beth reached into her purse and

pulled out her keys.

"We'll drop you off first," Lily protested.

Beth glanced at her watch. "No, it's in the opposite direction; you'll miss the start of the movie. I can walk, it's not far." In fact, when their parents had been alive, they used to walk every Sunday, weather permitting.

"I would offer you a ride, but mine is in the shop," Dean said, rising. "Ladies, thanks for allowing me to join you. Beth, I'll stop by one day this week to pick up the boxes for the charity drive. Call and let me know when it's convenient." When he picked up the ticket for the table, Beth protested. "Allow me." With a wink he ignored her and said his goodbyes. All this time, Beth was conscious of Razer's sharp gaze on her.

"We better be going," Lily announced. Lily and her friends got up then Lily walked to her sister and gave her a hug. "I'll be home by ten."

"Finish your project. Don't worry about the time, but remember you have school in the morning." Beth smiled at her, mischievously glancing at Charles.

"I will." Lily just stared at her. She was wearing a pale lilac dress with lace at the borders. It was soft and flowed to her knees. She looked like a model.

Beth got a lump in her throat as she reached out to give Lily's hand a quick squeeze. She would often touch Lily, noticing others close to her made excuses to do the same. Beth didn't take offense because she knew they did it for the same reason as her own; to reassure themselves that Lily was still within their reach. Women of less beauty had made fortunes with their looks, but they could not compare to Lily since it wasn't only her physical beauty that drew everyone in the room's eyes; her gentle spirit shone in her face and made her all the more radiant. Charles walked up, taking Lily's hand to hurry her towards the door.

Beth watched them go. Lily and Charles had grown up together. In fact, he lived just a couple of houses down from them and he was just as protective of Lily as she was, if not more so. He had loved Lily since he had first seen her introduced in her parents' church. When he placed an arm around Lily's shoulders as they went out the door, Lily casually moved away. She didn't return his feelings and never would.

Beth sighed and stood to leave the restaurant, still feeling the biker's gaze on her back. She was thinking that the walk home would help exercise off the chili cheese fries she had for lunch.

She hadn't gotten far when a shiny, black, monster of a truck pulled up next to her.

"Want a ride home?" Razer asked. The look on his face plainly said that he expected her to refuse.

"Yes." She firmly squashed her own internal voice that was asking what the hell she was doing. She was done being intimidated by them. Their behavior yesterday had been kind and Beth was not going to repay them with snobbery.

She moved to the other side of the truck as an expressionless man with the tattoos and wearing sunglasses jumped out, helping her into the front seat. He paused until she slid over to the middle of the seat before getting in next to her and firmly shutting the door. Razer then waited for her to buckle her seatbelt before moving back into the light traffic.

Beth self-consciously pulled down the cream skirt of her light dress to cover her thighs that had become exposed when she had slid into the truck.

"I live down Pine. It's just—"

"I know where it is." Beth nodded at his words. "That's Shade next to you and Train in the back."

"Hello." She turned to look at the men as they were introduced, receiving a nod from each. Beth guessed the one wearing the sunglasses was Shade, as every time she had seen him he had been wearing them on the only part of his body she was beginning to think wasn't tattooed. In the midst of the introductions, Beth wondered nervously who had decided on their nicknames.

"What's so funny?" Razer asked, seeing her smile.

Deciding to be honest, Beth confessed, "I was just wondering how you decided what your name was, if you chose it or someone else."

"Depends," Razer answered.

"On what?"

Razer shrugged. "A lot of things; it's usually because we're good at something."

"So because Shade wears sunglasses, he was given that name." Beth smiled.

"You think I'm called Shade because I wear sunglasses?" Beth felt his body shake in laughter next to her, and was instantly confused

"Then why do you think they call me Razer?"

"Because you like to shave?" Beth answered, noticing his cleanly shaven face, unlike his friends who seemed to like the shadowed look. This time loud laughter could be heard from the backseat.

Beth could see Razer fighting his own laughter. "Yeah, that's it."

Before Beth could figure out their laughter, the truck pulled into her driveway. Shade sat still while, this time, Razer jumped out.

"I'll help you down." He patiently held out his hand. As she unbuckled her seatbelt, she felt foolish trying to keep her skirt from flying up while holding her purse in her other hand. She slid toward his opened door where Razer held her hand until she regained her balance, shutting the door of the truck.

"Thanks for the ride."

"You're welcome." Razer followed as she walked to her door. Unlocking it, she turned to say goodbye, but before she could, he stopped her with a hand on her arm.

"I'm going for a ride on my bike for an hour or two; would you like to go?"

Beth looked toward the truck with the men inside.

"Just us. I'll go get my bike and you can get changed into some jeans."

"I can't—"

"Yes, you can. Your sister is gone for the day." At her surprised look, Razer appeared unapologetic at his obvious eavesdropping in the restaurant. "I bet you don't have anything important that has to be done today. Come for a ride with me in the mountains."

"All right." Beth found herself swayed by his smile. She was just as weak as the other women.

"Good. I'll be back in an hour. Be ready," he ordered.

Beth simply smiled at his order, going inside the house. Once the door closed, her calm exterior faded and the recriminations began in earnest. All the time she was getting changed into more comfortable clothes, she was determined to convey to him that she couldn't go when he returned. As she put on her tennis shoes then fixed her hair back into a tight ponytail, she continued to believe what she was telling herself.

When the knock came in less than the hour, Beth was surprised he was back so soon.

"That wasn't an hour," Beth accused when she opened the door.

"I was afraid you would change your mind."

"As a matter of fact—" Beth started to say.

"Oh, no, you don't. I didn't bust my balls to drive back here, breaking the speed limit, for you to turn me away. Where are your keys?"

"Wait just a minute. I—"

"Nope," Razer cut her off again and, seeing her keys sitting on the small table by the door, grabbed them, sliding them into his blue jeans' pocket. Beth swallowed apprehensively when her eyes were drawn towards him with his action.

"Let's go." Taking her hand, he pulled her out and locked the door.

31

Resigning herself to the point that this was indeed going to happen, Beth followed him meekly to his motorcycle.

"I have never ridden before," she told him nervously when he handed her a helmet before placing one on himself.

"It's not hard. Get on." Beth clumsily straddled the huge bike, holding on tight to the seat when Razer got on. "Grab on to my waist."

Beth nodded her understanding before reaching out and clutching him around his waist.

"No, Beth, like this." Reaching for her hands, he pulled them forward, scooting her whole body forward until the front of her body was plastered to his. Her arms held tightly to his waist. Without another word, he turned on the motor.

Beth's first motorcycle ride was an experience she would never forget. The mountains were beautiful in their full glory while the bike made her feel as if she could truly appreciate the natural beauty of their surroundings. She finally understood the freedom someone could feel, the excitement women were drawn to at the skill and strength to maneuver the beast of a machine around the turns as well as other cars on the road.

They rode for over an hour before they headed back to Beth's home. At her door, he pulled out her keys, unlocking the door before pulling it open.

"Would you like to come in for something to eat before you go home?"

"That's one of the things I never refuse."

"Oh, what else is on your list?" Beth teased, walking towards her kitchen.

Razer shrugged. "Not a lot, but home cooked food is definitely on the top."

"Well, let's see what I can do."

Beth opened her freezer, grabbing some Stromboli's that she'd made the previous weekend and then froze so that Lily could heat them when she arrived home from school. The freezer was full of pre-made meals that Lily could heat up for herself if one of the clients kept Beth late. Schedules were important to Lily and it kept things normal for her to have home cooked food in the oven instead of take-out.

The Stromboli's were filling the house with their delicious aroma as she made a salad and filled glasses of iced tea. Sitting them on the table, she motioned for Razer to take a seat.

"Sorry I don't have any beer."

"I didn't expect you to after your sister's reaction yesterday. Care to explain why she freaked out so badly?"

Beth hesitated. The whole town was aware Lily was adopted because her father had made a big production of it, however he had also never told anyone where he had found Lily. Beth didn't know how privy Razer was to the town gossip, nor did she want to disrespect her sister's privacy.

Beth answered hesitantly, "Lily has led a very sheltered life."

Opening the oven, she took out the Stromboli, serving one to Razer then one for herself.

"You haven't?" He waited until she took her seat before asking the question.

"I went away for college, spent four years in Lexington. I went through the partying stage, but Lily hasn't. She goes off to school in the fall."

"You're going to miss her." It wasn't a question.

"Yes, we're very close. I would even come home on the weekends just because I missed her so badly, but the college she's going to is just a few hours away. I plan to drive down a couple times a month. I don't want her driving home; she isn't the best of drivers. Treepoint is small and the roads are quiet, but busier roads give her trouble."

"Perhaps you should take her out driving on more

heavily traveled roads for the experience instead of trying to keep her from driving them."

"Tried that, took ten years off my life expectancy." Beth shuddered even now at the memory.

"That bad?"

"Worse."

Razer laughed at her expression. "She can't be that bad."

"Oh, yes, she can. She pulled out in front of a semi. It was a miracle he was able to swerve and miss us. If another car had been coming, I wouldn't be sitting here now."

Razer's laughter immediately died and they finished eating in silence. When they were done, they put their dishes in the sink. Not wanting Lily to see the dishes when she got home, Beth did the dishes while she heard Razer turn the television on. When she was done, she went into the living room to see Razer sprawled on her couch. Beth began to feel nervous being alone with him.

"Would you like some more tea?"

"No, thanks. Come watch this movie with me. The house is usually so loud I can't enjoy watching television anymore."

Beth moved to sit on the opposite end of the couch when Razer reached out and took her hand, pulling her down next to him.

"How many people live with you?" Beth questioned. She was curious; she knew nothing about his personal life. She didn't even know where he lived.

"It varies; sometimes twelve, sometimes thirty. Our club is pretty large and our headquarters are in Ohio. Members from there rotate in and out."

"It must be a pretty big house." Beth tried to think of houses in the surrounding areas with homes that large and couldn't think of one.

"It can be, although we always find enough room for everyone to sleep, even if we have to bunk together or sleep on the couch."

"I imagine that does make watching television difficult."

"Yeah. That, and we can never agree on the same thing."

They grew silent as they watched the movie. Partway through, Beth got up to go to the restroom and poured herself another iced tea. When she came back into the living room, she sat down, nervously reaching across Razer to place her drink on the side table. Razer watched her actions until she had sat settled down next to him without his prompting; her actions seemed stiff and uptight for a woman of her age.

"What?" Beth saw his puzzled frown.

"My grandmother doesn't act as uptight as you when the whole club shows up on her door. Aren't you a little young to be strung so tight?"

"I didn't mean to be," Beth replied defensively.

"Loosen up some. You act too old for your age. It's probably because you're working for all those old people you take care; it doesn't help."

"Are you insulting me or my job?"

"Both. I'm just saying act your age."

"Oh, how am I not acting my age?"

"Well for one, it wouldn't take me a whole day to kiss someone who wasn't so uptight."

"I am not uptight."

"You are."

"Am not."

"Prove it." Razer laughed at her prudishness.

"How?"

"Like this." Before Beth could determine his intentions, he had pulled her to him and kissed her. His mouth enveloped hers, seducing her with a single stroke of his tongue as it parted her lips, searching her mouth. Beth could taste the iced tea he had with dinner as she felt the heat, which she had never found in a kiss before. He was experienced, tempting her lips to open wider for him so that he could gain all the access he wanted without hesitation.

Beth's arms circled his shoulders as her hand delved into his long hair, finding the silkiness to be an irresistible sensation between her fingertips. His own hand buried into her hair and tilted her head backwards before his lips released hers to explore her sensitive throat. As he took a piece of skin into his mouth, he sucked it and produced a groan from Beth at the excitement it aroused.

Hearing it, Razer's hand slid across her stomach and underneath her thin t-shirt to skim over her lacy bra before gliding underneath to find her peaked nipple. Another moan escaped at the fire beginning to burn out of control in her body. Beth tried to regain control, she had never had trouble keeping it before, but lost it just as quickly when he lifted her shirt and pushed her bra out of the way.

Lowering his lips, he expertly began to suck on the nipple he had exposed while his other hand began to unsnap her jeans. Beth lifted her hands to stop him only to find that he had already stopped to take off his shirt. Beth watched, becoming aroused at the sight of his muscular chest. He didn't stop there; instead he unbuttoned his jeans, pulling his cock out. Blatantly, he took one of her hands and placed it on his hot length before wrenching her jeans down and sliding his fingers under the crotch of her panties to rub the rosy flesh underneath.

"That's it baby; get good and wet for me."

Beth sat stunned. Never had she been with a man who moved so fast through the steps of intimacy. The previous men she had dated had gone slowly, letting her set the pace. The only pace Razer was setting was one to see how many bases he could steal before sliding home.

Finding her clit, he began stroking until it started to throb in demand. Small whimpers escaped her trembling lips as Beth slowly moved her hands on his cock, wanting him to feel the passion at the level he was arousing within her body. She began to stroke him faster, unsure of herself and how he wanted to be touched.

"Like this." He wrapped his hand around hers and squeezed her fingers tighter around his hard length before then pumping her hand up and down in a rhythm he set for her. "I like it hard and rough." He forced her fingers to go even tighter on his cock and, when she took over, his hands returned to her cunt, sliding the panties out of the way so his long finger could slide deep within her.

His teeth bit her nipple, causing Beth's body to jerk when he added another finger, sliding deeper within her. "You're tight. I love tight pussy."

Beth was almost drawn out of the sexual haze he had thrown her into by his words, yet his finger was sliding through her wetness before adding another finger into her already tight sheathe, and her mind couldn't hold onto the reticence. Biting her nipple harder, he began to thrust his hips against her hands.

"Come here, baby." Sitting up, he pulled her jeans the rest of the way off, taking her panties with them.

"Wait." The burning arousal he had ignited was desperately trying to be doused by her conscious screaming at her to halt this before it was too late. Beth was trying to get her raging hormones under control, but found her body maneuvered until she was lying on his lap sideways with her leg draped over the back of the couch.

"It's cool. We don't have to fuck. Just let me play for a while." With his hand buried in her hair, he pulled her towards his cock. Without hesitation, Beth opened her mouth and took him, sucking hard while licking the tender underside.

His loud groan inflamed Beth; she once again reached out to hold his cock with her tight grip. While she alternatively sucked then stroked him, she could taste the leaking pre-cum on her tongue.

Razer's three fingers were buried deep within her once more while his thumb danced across her clit. This time it was her moans that filled the air as he built her towards an explosive climax. Beth tried to scream around his cock, but the hand that was gripping her hair forced her back down on his now spurting cock.

"Swallow it all." He kept his hand in her hair, rubbing her clit, giving her the full effect of her climax until his shaft quit twitching. When he finally released her hair, Beth rose up, not looking at him as she jerked her clothes back on.

"Beth?" Razer remained sitting with his jeans open, his semi hard length still hanging out.

"You better get dressed, Lily could be back anytime." Razer gave her a sharp look, but immediately shoved his member back into his jeans.

"What's the matter?" He tugged her down onto his lap after she was dressed.

Beth shook her head, blushing as she felt his hand smooth down her tumbled hair.

"I can see something is wrong. Are you regretting what we just did?"

"Yes." Beth was honest enough to admit to herself she had enjoyed it, however she couldn't help being disgusted with herself for giving in so easily to her body's demands. "It's just that I don't know you very well."

"I think you got to know me pretty well." Razer laughed. "Don't worry about all that other shit. It doesn't matter. I'm pretty easy to get to know. Besides, you already figured out how to make me happy."

Beth was disgruntled as she replied, "I think it's pretty obvious what makes you happy." The picture of him with his cock down the waitress's throat came unbidden to her mind.

Razer grinned, he knew women and it was obvious where her mind had gone. "Let me tell you a secret; it made me hotter than hell having you watching us. I imagined it was your mouth sucking me off and you didn't disappoint me tonight. I want your mouth again, but I want that tight pussy next. If it takes you getting to know me better, I can handle that. I enjoy your company. Now, does that sound good to you?"

"Okay," Beth said, determined not to wince at his plain talk. They were both adults; she would have to get over her prudish ways if she wanted to be with Razer.

"Good. Now, I gotta go or your sister is going to find me here and I don't think you want that."

"No." Beth apologized with her tone of voice.

"It's cool." He lifted her off his lap, taking her hand as he walked to the door. "Friday, we're having a party at the house. You want to come?"

"I would like that. Lily is going out of town with her youth group."

"I'll pick you up at eight. Sound good?"

"Yes." Then, with a light kiss on her lips, he was gone.

Beth stood uncertainly at the closed door before forcing herself to move upstairs to her room. Taking a short shower eased the tension, though not the desire that still plagued her body.

Beth thought about Razer as she sat on her bed, painting her toenails. She liked his easy nature and sense of humor. She had never been around someone like him before. He lightened that feeling of being stifled that she always walked around with and never seemed able to figure out how to solve. He made her feel free, as if she was capable of being like the other women her age who didn't have to worry about keeping so many people happy.

Beth thought back to the first time she had seen Razer, he had been across the street talking to the Sheriff. Her heart had done a flip in her chest, and every part of her body called to her to walk across the street and introduce herself. However, she hadn't been too afraid. Now she was determined to take that chance she hadn't that day.

The door opening and closing downstairs alerted Beth to Lily's return home. Not long after, there was a quiet knock on her door before Lily stuck her head inside.

"I'm just going to bed. Need anything?"

"No, thanks. Goodnight, Lily."

"Goodnight; sleep well."

"You, too."

CHAPTER FOUR

Mondays were always busy for Beth. Her first stop was Mrs. Langley, who was waiting for a ride to the beauty salon. Beth listened on the way as Mrs. Langley gave a list of groceries for Beth to pick up. She was expecting Vincent Bedford and Samantha to be coming to dinner that evening, so she would be preparing a meal. Beth would fit the grocery shopping into her tight schedule, hoping this time the father and daughter would actually show up. The last time they hadn't shown without as much as a courtesy phone call to cancel.

It didn't take long for her to drop Mrs. Langley off at the salon. Then, her next stop was Ton's home. He lived on the outskirts of town, a couple miles up Pine Mountain. Beth always enjoyed the drive and Mr. James gave her money for gas. The log cabin, which was Ton's home, suited him. It was rustic and old fashioned with hardwood floors; built on the ridge to capture the beauty of the mountains through the windows on the front of the house.

Ton answered her first knock, so he must have heard her arrival. Her smile was returned with a sheepish one. Beth had not seen him since his drunken rampage at *Rosie's*.

Upon entering, he didn't prevaricate. "I'm sorry Beth. My behavior was inexcusable." He poured her a cup of strong black coffee. "Have a seat."

Beth sat, picking up the coffee and wincing at the taste. Ton pushed the sugar towards her and she hastily added several spoonfuls to make it drinkable.

"I have your groceries in the car."

"I don't know why Loker won't let me do my own shopping. The drive isn't that far from town."

"Probably because you're blind in one eye," Beth gently reminded him.

"Yes, well, I remember where everything is. I still see perfectly fine." Beth shuddered in horror at his reply. "Doesn't matter anyway. Loker took my keys after *Rosie's*. He even threatened the cab company if they came out here to pick me up."

"I'm sorry," she said softly.

"Don't be. Guess I brought it on myself. I just go in for a couple drinks and then, before I know it, I'm drinking the harder stuff. Guess I'm not doing so well adjusting to being old with nothing to do." He ran his gnarled hand through his long, grey hair.

"You need a hobby," Beth suggested.

"That I do, drinking isn't working out so good at being one." Beth laughed. She found it hard to believe the mean, foul-mouthed man she had seen last Thursday was the same one standing before her now.

"Well, I better get the groceries packed in before you go. I know you have other clients to see about."

"I do, but I have a few things I wanted to get done here first, if you don't mind. I scheduled in a couple hours and I don't want to lose the money."

"You sure you're not staying because you and that son of mine think I can't take care of myself?"

"Not at all. I need all the hours I can get with a sister to put through college. It can be very expensive." Ton tried to stare her down, but Beth held firm. Twenty-seven years in the military and he caved to a blue-eyed blond. Of course, Ton realized there could be worse things than looking at Beth clean his house for a couple of hours, which definitely softened the blow.

"Well, I don't want to deprive anyone of their education."

"We both would appreciate it."

"Okay then, what did you have in mind?"

"A little of this and a little of that. Go pack in the groceries while I start a load of laundry."

By the time Beth finished three hours later, she left behind a stupefied Ton standing in his clean living room that smelled of the sweet scent from the laundry. She completely cleaned his entire home, including fresh sheets and blankets on his bed. His still wet, freshly washed hair had not even been spared; she had firmly sat him down at the table, taking scissors and a comb to it until he looked better than he had in several weeks.

Beth returned to town, picking up groceries for two other clients, plus the additional ones Mrs. Langley had requested to be purchased. She then rushed to meet her at the diner next to the beauty salon where Mrs. Langley was to have had lunch with a friend until Beth's return.

After dropping the beautified Mrs. Langley at home, Beth had three more clients to see before she could call it a day. Each client had their own set of chores that needed to be completed, plus several that were spur of the moment requests. She always tried to do the additional items if at all possible, not wrapping up her day until late. When she finally arrived home, she found Lily doing homework. She ate a quick dinner and headed for bed, already dreading the work that was looming during the coming week.

By the time Friday arrived, Beth was exhausted. After putting Lily on the church bus with a caution to be careful and a tearful hug, she watched the bus drive off before going home to take a nap. She woke a couple of hours before Razer was due to pick her up, took a long shower and then blow dried her hair before putting on light make-up and getting dressed in jeans along with a pretty red top that softly clung to her full breasts. This time, Beth was ready when Razer knocked on time.

"You look great. Ready?"

"Yes." Beth removed a jacket from the closet and followed Razer out to where Razer's motorcycle was parked.

Beth felt more comfortable getting on the bike now, and sliding her arms tightly around Razer. She was excited to see where he lived, but nervous about meeting his friends. She had never put herself in this position. Even in college, what few parties she had attended had been with the one or two girlfriends she had made who hadn't minded her straight laced ways. Just once, Beth wanted to be reckless, to live as other women did and not hear her father's sermons in her mind about what others considered normal. How could she teach Lily freedom if she wasn't willing to find it for herself?

Beth was shocked when Razer pulled up and parked. She got off the bike, staring. "You guys are staying at Stolmes factory?"

The factory had been built four years ago when the economically depressed area had tried desperately to find work for the people in Treepoint. A businessman, Gavin Stolmes, had come to town and bought a huge amount of property that everyone considered useless. It had been over forested, steep and rocky. It wasn't even a particularly pretty piece of land. The saving grace about the property was that it was a large acreage and that had been the selling point to Stolmes. He and his private investors, which included several of the local businessmen, had put up the money and built the factory in record time. The factory was completed and the machinery had been ordered, but it never arrived. Stunned, the investors discovered that Stolmes had left town without a word, taking the two million needed to buy the machines to build the equipment that the plant had been laid out to build. There even had been a bed and breakfast built next to the factory to house the buyers when they visited and it easily held the group of Razer's associates.

"Yeah."

The house was lit up inside and music could be heard out on the front yard where groups of people were standing around, drinking various forms of liquor.

"Let's go." Taking her hand, he led her up the steps to the front porch, which was crammed with even more people than Beth had first thought.

"You didn't tell me there would be this many people here."

"It's busy this weekend. The guys are up from Ohio. We're all headed back next week. A dispute has broken out; Viper wants to send a message."

"What message?"

"A don't fuck-with-me message."

"Oh."

He opened the door, ushering her inside and into another world. Beth thought it would be people standing around drinking, talking and dancing. A normal party, but there was nothing normal about this party. They were doing much more than she had ever imagined.

Women were all over the place in different stages of undress; some dancing, some sitting, yet all of them were in various stages of sexual acts.

Beth came to a hard stop. "Whoa! I think I misunderstood what kind of party this is. I can't stay here."

Razer grabbed her around the waist, stopping her panicked flight. "Calm down. Nothing is going to happen that you're not ready for or you don't want to do."

"You said a party, not an orgy. And I can tell you now I am not ready for this party." Beth tried to lower her scandalized voice, aware of the curious eyes staring at her in amusement.

"Beth, you said you partied in college?" Razer

questioned.

"Yes, normal frat parties. This is like a frat party on steroids."

"Come on. It's not that bad."

"It's bad, real bad," Beth said in a low voice as she watched a pretty blond writhing in desire on Knox's lap as he sucked on her bared breasts.

"Beth, we are quite a bit older than college kids. I assumed when you said you had partied that extended beyond the college age range. Give it a chance." After seeing the couple Beth's eyes were glued on, Razer continued, "Ignore that. Let's get a drink."

Beth felt like throwing up from being so nervous. She no longer merely heard her father's words in her mind; now there were screaming words, dire warnings of hell and brimstone.

Razer grabbed a couple of beers, handing her one before pulling her down on his lap on an overstuffed leather chair. Train was seated on the couch beside it with a woman on each side of him. One seemed to be licking his ear while another was bobbing up and down on his cock.

At this point, Beth knew she was well out of her depth. In fact, she was trying to devise a way of telling Razer to get her the hell out of there when Evie appeared.

"Hey, Beth."

"Hello, Evie." Beth looked at her, not wanting her eyes to return to Train as she heard his groans of completion. Beth eyed the outfit Evie was wearing, trying not to appear flustered at the tight pair of shorts that barely covered the curve of her butt and a top that was unbuttoned to show her firm breasts.

Beth felt overdressed, but wasn't about to rectify the situation. She took a swallow of the beer, trying to calm herself down. Razer's hand started to rub her back, easing the fear threatening to have her running out of the room.

"I can see from your face that Razer didn't warn you

the parties can get a little wild."

"No, he didn't."

Evie laughed and sat down on the arm of the chair they were sitting on. "I have been partying since I was fifteen. I was twenty-one the first time I came to one of their parties, and it still shocked me."

Razer and Train started talking, both ignoring the women at their side. "You'll get used to it. The next time you come it won't be such a surprise," Evie sympathized with the obviously overwhelmed newcomer.

"I doubt that." Beth sincerely was thinking that once she got out of here, she would never be back.

Evie laughed as if reading her mind. Trying to ease her fears, she changed the topic, "I like your top. All my pretty ones have disappeared. These bitches just borrow without asking, so we simply wash the clothes and everyone grabs something clean. The shorts are different, not many can get their fat asses into mine."

"I bet not." Evie was small, probably a one or two. Beth was one of the fat asses they wouldn't fit.

"Not everyone likes skin and bones," Razer said, rubbing Beth's ass. "I happen to like mine with a little jiggle."

"Never notice you complain when you were humpin' it," Evie joked back. She caught the shocked look on Beth's face and instantly regretted her ill-conceived joke.

"Damn, girl. I didn't mean anything." Beth gave her a false smile at her apology.

"The first couple of times I saw Razer, he had a different woman hanging on him. I just didn't realize you two had a history."

"No history," Evie said. "How about we change the subject? Razer was telling me what you do; I bet that's interesting."

Beth looked in her eyes and saw a sincere desire to be friends. She liked the girl and, as all the friends she had made had gotten married or left the small town for greener pastures, she wanted to become friends as well.

"What do you do?" Beth asked.

"I was a nurse in Ohio. I applied here at the local hospitals and the two doctor's offices, but they haven't called."

"You're a nurse?" Evie stiffened at Beth's surprised tone.

"You don't think I look like a nurse?"

Beth burst out laughing, stopping when she saw the hurt look Evie tried to hide. Razer's arm tightened around her waist, letting her know he was also unhappy. Even Train was throwing her a dirty look.

"Well, to be honest, right now a nurse wouldn't be my first clue as to your profession." Beth waved her hand at Evie's open top. "But you misunderstood me; if any of my male clients saw you, they would go into cardiac arrest." This time, everyone burst out laughing. "Seriously, I have a nursing degree also. I worked and got my masters in business with a minor in accounting. Before everyone can say I'm flaunting my degrees, I am just telling you this because I have been getting a little overwhelmed with all the work I've been contracted to do. I was thinking of hiring someone part-time, if you think you might be interested?"

"God, yes. I have been bored out of my mind stuck here all day with the other girls. I don't want full-time, whatever hours you could give me would be great," She hastily added before Beth could reply.

Beth frowned. "Perhaps I should have mentioned you would need a car. Do you have one?"

"Yes, and it's in good shape."

"Have you got your phone handy?"

Evie pulled a small cell phone out of her back pocket. Beth took it and programmed her number into it then pulled her own cell phone out, adding Evie to her contact list.

"Give me a call on Monday. I'll work something out

this weekend on what hours I can offer."

A loud booming voice yelled Evie's name from the upstairs. "Gotta go before Knox comes looking for me." Beth turned to see Knox and the blond woman waiting for Evie at the top of the stairs. When Evie reached them, Knox placed an arm around their shoulders before moving out of Beth's sight.

"That was nice of you."

"I had a rough week. I need the help and honestly, should have hired someone a month ago. This will give me more time to spend with Lily before she leaves for college and someone to cover for me in emergencies when I go visit."

"Works out nice for you both."

Beth only nodded because, while they had been talking, he had turned her sideways on his lap, facing away from Train. His hand was now running up and down her thigh, his thumb casually brushing her denim-covered mound before sliding away. The sensation was teasing her into wanting it to linger longer. Almost the instant that occurred to her, one of his hands buried itself into her long hair, tilting her head back and kissing her before she could protest. When his lips touched hers, all thoughts of objection vanished. There was just something so naughty about sitting on his lap and letting him pet her.

Razer sucked her tongue into his mouth, wanting to see if she would be able to respond to him in the heavily crowded room. Beth dragged her nails over his t-shirt covered chest. She was forgetting where she was and getting into the moment when Razer broke away.

"Let's go." Razer tore his lips away.

"Where to?"

"My room. I don't think you're ready to fuck in public yet and, if you keep scratching at me with those nails, I am tearing those jeans off you." Standing up, he pulled her up on her feet.

Razer hustled her through the crowd and up the long

flight of steps.

"Razer…"

He opened the second door at the top and led her inside. His lips found hers before she could say anything as he kicked the door shut behind them. Beth was still trying to make up her mind if this was really what she wanted.

"Baby, you're so hot."

The trite phase that was something he probably had said to several women since hitting puberty was exactly what she needed to bring herself to her senses.

"Razer slow down." She pushed him away and put her hands up to ward him off. "Can we slow down a minute?"

Razer frowned. "Do you think I'm pressuring you?"

"No! I'm not saying that at all. I just need to catch my breath for a minute."

"I can do that." He smiled and reached for her again, pulling her into his body to rub her back.

"Look, if this isn't working for you, I can take you home. I can see how it can be a little much. I'm used to this way of life, but I can also see how it can be for someone else."

"You understand?" Beth gave him a sweet smile. "I just feel a little overwhelmed."

"That's cool. We can try another night. Maybe we can catch a movie when I get back from Ohio."

"I'd really like that."

"Good. Now, let's get out of here before my good intentions go out the window."

The trip down the stairs was much slower. Razer was being incredibly nice; Beth couldn't believe that he didn't at least try to change her mind. It made her feel as if he was beginning to want to know her better, maybe he hoped to form a relationship with her in the future. The ride back was gloomy after all the excitement of the night had been anti-climatic. Beth consoled herself that at least she had tried versus not trying at all.

At her door, he kissed her again, drawing a response

that she couldn't control. "Would you like to come in?"

Razer's lips slid reluctantly away from her neck. "I better not. We'll be leaving early and, if I leave now, I can grab a few hours sleep. I'll call you when I get back."

"All right. Have a safe trip." Beth watched from her doorway as he drove away, contrarily wishing she had remained at his house. Her fear had won the battle, making her run like a scared little mouse. Again.

She was getting in her bed, going over the night as she slowly became sick to her stomach that Razer would be returning to a house full of half-naked women. He hadn't been worried about getting up early in the morning before she chickened out. The more she thought about it, the sicker she felt to her stomach. She didn't want him to turn to another woman because she had been too chicken to sleep with him.

Before she could change her mind, she jumped out of bed, hastily dressed in a pair of jeans and a t-shirt, grabbed her car keys and headed back towards the house.

Arguing with herself the whole way back, she sat in her car for several minutes before gathering enough courage to get out of the car. Hopefully, he wasn't asleep yet and, if he were, she would wake him up in a way he would never forget.

The party had become even louder, if that were possible. Some of the attendees were even having sex on the couch with others yelling encouragement. Beth didn't think she would ever get used to the things she had seen that night. She looked around the room, relieved that Razer wasn't locked in the embrace of one of the women, her confidence was boosted at the thought that he had come home and gone to bed as he had said he would. Beth went up the stairs to his room and raised her hand to knock, not wanting to walk in unannounced. Her confidence faded as she wondered whether he would be happy to see her at his door this late.

"Well, well… if it isn't little Miss Goody two shoes."

Sam's low voice drew her hand away from the door. She was barely covered in a blue see-through nightie that Beth could only imagine had been sold in a sex shop.

"You don't have to knock, come in and join the party. I just left to get the lube." Raising her hand with a tube of ointment in it, she blatantly wiggled it in front of Beth's stunned face.

"The more, the merrier, Razer always says." Sam gave Beth a sly grin. "I'm surprised you came back. Razer can be a little hard to satisfy, but I'm sure you know that since you haven't accomplished it either time you went out with him. I took the hit for you last week; he fucked me all night long after he left you. I could hardly walk the next day." Sam was telling the truth, Beth could tell by her smug grin. Razer had obviously discussed what they had done at Beth's house with Samantha.

"Couldn't do it tonight, girl. I had to get help."

Before Beth's stunned mind could function, Sam opened the bedroom door. Beth's gaze was drawn inside as the woman had cruelly intended. Razer was in bed with Evie lying on top, his large cock buried in her pussy while Train fucked her from behind, pinning Evie between their thrusting bodies. Even Knox was in there, sitting on the chair by the rocking bed with his fist pumping his hard dick.

"Well, come on in. I'm back boys and I brought company," Sam smugly announced.

Beth turned and ran, almost tripping down the steps, barely managing to grasp the handrail in time. She kept going, running even when Razer yelled her name.

Beth knew it was only her years in track that allowed her to sprint to her car, although she wasn't certain why she had even run. She had already made a fool of herself and it wasn't like he had been in any position to run after her. Tears were falling down her cheeks. Beth couldn't believe how naïve she had been. Even last week, after he had left her with the taste of him, he had come back here to fuck Sam.

She had wanted freedom from the strict rules her father had ingrained in her since childhood, wanting to test herself, but what she had done was throw herself into hurricane waters. She had thought she would be able to swim, instead she had been torn apart. Razer was out of her league and she had known that all along. After all, he was very sexual; living in a club environment that provided easy access to women without the usual complications. Coping with a woman who placed sexual limitations on a relationship wouldn't have even occurred to him.

Beth didn't even bother turning on the lights when she walked into her house where she found her way in the dark to the kitchen. Grabbing bottled water, she sat at her kitchen table. She had just buried her head in her hands when her cell phone rang, the caller I.D said Evie calling. Beth knew it wasn't Evie calling, that it was Razer instead. Her lips twisted into a self-deprecating sneer; he had never bothered to even ask for her phone number.

Brushing the tears away, Beth gathered every bit of pride her parents had instilled within her and picked up the phone.

"Hello?"

"Beth, I never meant for you to walk into something like that. I knew you weren't ready to—"

"I would never be ready for something like that, Razer, nor would I want to."

Beth could hear his sigh of frustration over the phone. "Look, I can be there in twenty minutes. We can talk—"

She cut him off. "Don't bother. Sam made it perfectly clear to me, but I do have a quick question before I hang up; did you have any intention of calling me when you got back in town?"

The silence that met her question shredded her last bit of self-respect.

"Listen, Beth, I think that we're on different wavelengths. Sam told me you've been with several guys from town while you yourself told me you partied in college. I thought you knew the score, so I was willing to play your game, but woman, you're just too much work for a piece of pussy."

Each word flayed her soul. She had been planning on a relationship, one that might not even have lasted, but he hadn't even wanted that, just another fuck toy. She tuned back in to hear him finish.

"I am sorry that you walked into that. I wanted it to end with no hard feelings."

Beth was done, she hung up. Sam had lied, convincing Razer she was experienced and setting Beth up for failure. Although, Beth had to admit to herself that she was also at fault. The attraction she had felt for Razer had pushed her to do things that her common sense had told her was too soon. If she had wanted a romantic relationship, then a sexy biker was not where she should have looked. Fortunately, Beth knew someone who wouldn't mind her inexperience; he wanted the same type of relationship she needed in her life.

* * *

Beth kept herself busy with cooking and cleaning for the rest of the weekend. When Sunday finally arrived, she had breakfast ready when Lily walked in the door. Lily laughed at the tight hug Beth gave her.

"I was only gone two nights."

Seeing Beth's pale face, Lily's smile disappeared. "Have you been sick?"

"No, I'm fine. I was in one of my moods to cook and I just overdid it. The good news is, we have enough dinners frozen for the next two months." Lily laughed in relief then told her about the youth group's trip as they readied for church.

During the sermon, Beth paid particular attention to the Pastor's appearance. She had certainly noticed before that he was a handsome man with light brown hair cut closely to his head. He was also tall and well built; both of which were surprising for a man of his profession. Beth seemed to remember that he had been in the military as a chaplain; in fact, he had served two tours ministering to the soldiers overseas.

When he had first arrived in Treepoint, he had made friendly overtures, but Beth had politely turned him down. She had no intention of finding herself in her mother's shoes; however, the more Beth listened to him, the more she appreciated how he was teaching God's word with more modern expectations.

After the service, Beth for once waited patiently for her sister to finish talking to her friends. Noticing the Pastor had finally finished saying his goodbyes to the parishioners and was gathering the papers on the podium, Beth stepped forward as Pastor Dean passed the pew where she had been sitting.

"How are you this Sunday, Beth?"

"Just fine, Pastor Dean. I hope your trip was successful."

"Yes, we were able to lay a good foundation to rebuild the structure. The congregation should be able to finish the repairs."

"I'm glad to hear it." Once again he started to walk towards the doorway outside. "Pastor Dean, Lily and I would like you to come for dinner Friday night if you're not busy."

The Pastor came to a sudden stop with a speculative look in his eyes. "I would enjoy taking you up on that invitation. Would six be fine?"

Beth smiled, relieved at his interested response. "That sounds perfect."

* * *

Monday morning was hurried as both Beth and Lily had overslept. She was about to leave for work after Lily left for school with Charles, who picked her up every morning since earning his license, when the doorbell rang. Already in a rush, Beth answered the door with a frown and was surprised to see Evie standing nervously on her doorstep, wearing a pretty blue pair of scrubs.

"I know you probably won't hire me now, but I really need the job," she said with a hesitant smile.

Beth stepped back, opening her door further for her to enter. She knew that she would never get the picture of her sandwiched between Razer and Train out of her mind, yet she was also aware that it was her problem, not Evie's.

"I still need help. Your private life is your own and none of my business," Beth answered her quietly.

"Razer and I are just—"

Beth cut her reply short, "Again, it's none of my business. I just have one request; if you are going to work for me, don't ever mention him to me again. Can you do that?"

"Yes, but—"

Again, Beth cut her short. "Good. Now it seems you want to start today and that works for me. Monday's are a killer. I hope you can provide me with a couple of references that I can check out."

"No problem."

"Good. Let's go. Today you can drive with me until you learn the clients and where they live."

"Anything you say, boss," Evie said with a grin.

CHAPTER FIVE

Nine months later

Blake was coming down Mrs. Langley's staircase as Beth finished cleaning the large living room. Glancing over her shoulder, she saw him balancing two large boxes.

"Need any help?"

"No, thanks. I can handle it." He sat the heavy boxes down on the floor. "I packed away all the Christmas decorations, cleaned the attic and threw away everything Mrs. Langley told me to. These two weren't labeled. She said for you to go through them and organize whatever is inside if it's important."

"I don't have time to right now, I have a date with Dean tonight. Could you put them in the trunk of my car as you leave?"

"No, problem. Anything else before I go?"

"No, that's all for today. See you next week."

Beth went to the kitchen to make a small meal for Mrs. Langley before she also left for the day; a bowl of warm soup, a glass of cold milk and several homemade cookies on a small tray. Beth had made the cookies last night before going to bed.

Carefully carrying it upstairs to Mrs. Langley's bedroom, she found the woman lying in bed, watching her favorite show. Beth helped her sit up before placing the tray on her lap.

"Thank you. Are those chocolate chunk cookies?"

"Yes. I left a container of them on the kitchen counter for later."

"They are my favorite," she said while picking one up and biting into it.

"I will have to remember that." Beth smiled and chatted with her about the medical program she was watching as she cleaned the room.

"Have you seen Samantha lately?" Mrs. Langley asked as Beth took away the empty tray.

"No, I haven't," Beth lied, remorseless. No way would she be drawn into a conversation about the woman's granddaughter. Samantha was constantly seen around town with the members of The Last Riders. Beth had seen her several times herself since that night months ago. Twice on the back of Razer's bike where, each time, Sam had manage to throw a gloating look, if not giving her the finger.

"She didn't come by for Christmas. Vincent explained she was busy working and would visit when she had the time. Perhaps if you happen to see her, you might mention her grandmother would enjoy a visit."

Beth forced a smile. "If I see her, I will be happy to pass along your message."

"Good. Now you better be going. You don't want to be late for your date."

"I won't. I'll come by tomorrow to tell you all about it." Beth smiled as she heard the television volume increase when she left the room.

Beth washed and cleaned the dirty dishes before leaving. She was only paid to work for two days a week, however, since Beth had noticed Mrs. Langley losing weight, she made sure to stop by daily to fix a nutritious meal and that it was in fact, eaten. Hopefully, Samantha would take pity on her grandmother and visit soon. If not,

Beth would keep her word and broach the subject the next time the selfish girl was near.

* * *

"Beth, Pastor Dean is here!" Beth grimaced at Lily's manners. She had come home for the Christmas holiday and would be going back in two weeks.

Picking up her sweater, she went downstairs to meet Dean.

"Wow, you look great," Evie exclaimed as she looked up from the groceries she was organizing into boxes to be delivered the next day. Her car had broken down outside Beth's home when she had dropped the groceries off, so she had set to work while waiting for one of the members from the club to pick her up.

"Thanks." Beth was wearing a new royal-blue, tight skirt that ended above the knees with a matching sweater that had horizontal blue and black stripes that emphasized her breasts and small waist as it clung snugly to her curves. Every time she moved, the bare expanse of her stomach teased the eye. The large, black belt and sky-high heels that touched off the outfit had her feeling sexy and provocative. Not the best two combinations when her date was with the local pastor.

Beth saw Dean standing by the door.

"Hi." Giving him a welcoming smile, she walked across the room to greet him. As Beth's arms slid seductively around his shoulders to brush his mouth with hers, Dean's lips returned the light pressure. His arms then came around her, pulling her body close.

"I've finished with the groceries, so I'll be going since my ride is here," Evie said, closing the last box.

Beth turned in Dean's arms to see Razer sitting in the chair. This wasn't the first time she had seen him since that embarrassing night; she had become adept at dealing with the occasions. Thankfully, he was out of town frequently and Evie had kept to her word to never mention him.

Carefully hiding her reaction, she greeted him before

turning back to Evie. "Thanks, Evie, let me know if your car can't be repaired by tomorrow and I'll reschedule your clients."

"Shouldn't be a problem. Razer is a genius with machinery," Evie said.

"Then I will see you tomorrow. Lily, I'll be back in a few hours." Lily waved them away, engrossed in a book as she sat at the table. Dean and Beth left with Razer, Evie following closely behind.

As they came up to Dean's car, he held the door open as she slid inside the modest car.

"It's working out well? Her working for you?" he asked when he was sitting behind the wheel.

Dean drew her attention away from watching Razer raising the hood of Evie's car.

"Yes. It couldn't have worked out better," Beth answered honestly.

"It doesn't bother you that she lives with a large group of men in a motorcycle club. Some of your clients are fairly well-off."

"I trust Evie, and I think of her as a good friend. Besides, just because they're a motorcycle club doesn't automatically mean they are criminals," Beth defended Evie heatedly, unconsciously including The Last Riders.

"I wasn't criticizing. I like her, too." Dean raised a hand in surrender.

"You do?"

"Yes."

"Good. Now where are we eating? I'm starved."

* * *

Dean looked up from his practically completed sermon when Razer walked in his open office door.

"I guess miracles do happen," Dean said, leaning back in his chair.

Razer put his hands in his pockets as he headed over to the window beside the desk to stare outside. "How have you been doing?" Razer asked without responding to

Dean's comment.

"Very well. I've got a good church, a good woman and good friends. What more could a man ask for?" Dean noticed Razer's stiffened body, yet he didn't bring it up.

"You've been here a while Razer and you're just now stopping by. Is there a reason?"

"Thought I'd stop by for a chat."

Dean sighed and brought up the subject that Razer was dancing around. "I saw you two together. I was at a parishioner's home in the neighborhood and saw her on your bike. That was the same weekend she asked me out." Dean glanced down to see Razer's hands clenching into fists. "I had made a play for her when I first got to town; she turned me down flat. After that night with you, she ran straight into my arms. You must have scared the hell out of her."

"She knew what I wanted and she wanted me to work for it. It wasn't worth the effort," Razer weakly argued.

Dean stood and walked around the desk, casually leaning back against it.

"Oh, she's worth it. Isn't that what you're here to ask me? If you made a mistake? For Christmas, I gave Beth a weekend trip to Vegas. She's never been out of Kentucky her whole life. I'm going to ask her to marry me that weekend, Razer."

"Everyone at the club will be happy for you. Guess that answers my questions on how life is treating you. Let me know when you set a date. I'll send a present. See you around." Razer turned towards the door.

Dean almost let him go, but he owed the man his life. It was time to pay him back. "Evie has started coming to church on Sundays, did she tell you?" Before he could answer, Dean continued, "She told me what happened that night. She feels pretty bad about it. She likes Beth. She also told me about the bullshit that Sam has been mouthing off about Beth. I thought you were smarter than to listen to a jealous bitch. Unlike you, I cared enough to find out about

Beth. I talked to people that care about her; the people she sits next to every Sunday. Do you know she has never missed a Sunday service, even after her father, who was the previous pastor, had passed?"

Razer turned back, not saying anything, only listening. "The congregation loves her and, when they found out I was dating her, they couldn't tell me her virtues fast enough. If you hadn't been a jackass to her that night, she would never have dated me. Her father was a miserable bastard who controlled every aspect of Beth's life, so she was never allowed to play and socialize as other kids her age were. They never even had a television; he considered it the Devil's medium. They read scripture every night; her whole world was the church. I watched a videotape of him giving a sermon and he even scared me. There is no way she would place herself back in such a stifling environment if you hadn't scared her so badly."

"Sam told me she had dated several boys in high school, and Beth told me she had partied in college," Razer defended himself.

"Beth wasn't allowed to date in high school, she never attended extra-curricular activities and she never attended dances or prom. She won't even dance with me; she's too embarrassed to admit she doesn't know how. His congregation told her father every misstep Beth made. If she even talked to a boy, they told him. I imagine if she attended a beer bust in college, Beth considered it partying. She probably was too embarrassed to admit to you how little she was exposed to, even if you gave her the opportunity," Dean said intuitively. "Since she graduated college and became Lily's guardian, you were the first one to manage to get close to her. She works long hours to pay for all of Lily's expenses and has managed to pay off almost all the debt her parents left. She didn't want Lily to lose her home."

"I should have known she was inexperienced," Razer said in self-recrimination.

Dean nodded. "I can only determine that she was attracted to you and was willing to take a chance, despite every stricture her father had droned into her since birth."

"She must have thought she walked into Sodom and Gomorrah that night."

"That may be, however, Beth and Evie have become best friends. She doesn't even hold a grudge against Samantha. I am willing to bet she would forgive you if you tried."

Razer shook his head. "I don't fit into her life and she damn sure doesn't fit into mine."

"Evie tells me you have been nailing every woman that's looked your way the last nine months, Razer. Yet you haven't touched Evie or Sam since that night. You can drink all the beer you want, but if it is water you want, nothing will quench your thirst."

"Don't preach to me."

"I'm done," Dean said, straightening from the desk. "I'm going to pay back my debt to you. I am giving you until this weekend to take another shot at a woman I have come to care about. Beth will make me the perfect wife other than the fact that I think she fell in love with you first. The man I served with, who saved my life and was like a brother to me, would be smart enough to figure out a way to get the best of both worlds."

CHAPTER SIX

Razer sat his empty beer bottle down on the bar, trying not to think about Beth and Dean's trip to Vegas tomorrow.

"Want another?" Mick asked.

"No, going home."

"Since when do you drink one beer and leave?"

The slamming door had everyone's eyes turning towards the noise.

Loker James came striding angrily to the bar.

"Mick, have you seen Ton? I just got back in town this morning and when I went home, both him and the truck were gone."

"I haven't seen him today."

"Mother-fucker! I am going to strangle him with my bare hands when I find him." The ringing of his cell phone cut off further threats of violence.

The expression on his face had everyone unashamedly listening. Through the phone call, Loker was mostly silent; so they didn't get many clues. However, Loker's face turned white and his hand was shaking as he ended the conversation.

"I found Ton."

Razer and Mick exchanged glances. They knew the news was bad.

"He was in an accident. He broadsided Beth Cornett's car on Ivy Hill. They've both been taken to the E.R."

Razer's hand gripped the rail of the bar, his shaking knees were barely holding him upright where he stood.

"How bad is she hurt?" Two sets of eyes turned to him in surprise at his reaction.

"Don't know. That was the only information dispatch would tell me. The sheriff told them to contact me and to have me meet him at the hospital."

Loker left without another word, jogging to his car. He was putting the car in gear when the passenger side door was wrenched open and Razer jumped in.

"What the fuck are you doing?"

"Going with you."

"Why?"

"Beth." Without further question, Loker floored the gas pedal.

By the time Loker reached the hospital, there were six bikers that had been in the bar when Razer ran out who were now following behind. Curiosity had gotten them on their bikes to follow.

Loker went directly to the ER with Razer close on his heels. As he entered through the sliding doors, he could already hear the commotion Ton was making in a nearby room. He was too relieved that his father was in good enough condition to be enraged with the nurse loosened the knot his gut had been twisted into.

"Let me go, woman, I have to check on that little girl."

"Sir, I told you that the sheriff is checking. When he comes back in a few moments, he'll relay the information on the girl's condition." Ton was trying to jump out of a wheelchair while the middle-aged nurse was unsuccessfully trying to keep him seated. "I need to check your injuries."

"I'm fine. They checked me out in the ambulance. It's that poor girl who needs help."

"Dad," Loker spoke, trying to get Ton's attention.

Ton faced his son with tears streaming from his eyes. It was a tough sight for Loker to see; his hard ass father never showed emotions that he would consider weak.

"I know what you're going to say, but I am not drunk, haven't had a drink all day. I was just going to the store for a pack of cigarettes. A pack of cigarettes that probably cost that girl her life. There was blood everywhere." Ton lifted his shaking hands to cover his face. "I saw her, too. She pulled right out in front of me, but I couldn't stop in time."

"Ton." Loker tried to quiet his father, worried that he would incriminate himself.

"No. I hurt that girl. I want you to shoot me."

"How is she?" Razer asked quietly from his position of leaning against the pale yellow wall with Shade, Knox and Rider standing beside him.

"They won't tell me." Ton redoubled his efforts to get out of the wheelchair.

"Ton, stop." The soft voice coming from the doorway had everyone turning. Razer thought he was imagining her voice, however as he turned, it was clearly Beth with tear-swollen eyes and trembling lips, clutching her purse in fear. Razer might have felt a surge of joy at seeing Beth was okay, but it was short-lived as the realization sunk in that it had been Lily behind the wheel instead.

"I am so sorry, Beth. I didn't think…" Ton's voice faded off as he immediately stopped his struggles.

They waited for Beth to let Ton have it. Lily was Beth's only family and everyone in town knew how Beth protected and worshiped her baby sister.

As Beth walked forward to face the crying man, no one moved to stop her. She reached out and, instead of the smack everyone expected, cupped his beard-roughened cheek, gently brushing his tears away.

"You have to calm down. Remember your blood pressure. You don't want me to be worried about you, too, do you?"

"No." Ton tried to gain control under Beth's steady gaze.

"Has he been checked out?" Beth asked the nurse.

"Not yet. He wouldn't let me."

"Go with her, Ton. As soon as I find out Lily's condition, I'll find you." Ton nodded, squeezing her hand.

The nurse ushered Ton towards a room and, not long after, a door halfway down the hall opened. Everyone froze expectantly as the Sheriff walked out. He looked at the audience waiting for news as Beth instantly moved to his side.

"How is she?"

"Lucky. She has a concussion, a sprained ankle and she is going to be sore as hell for a couple of days, but all that research you put into purchasing a safe car paid off."

The Sheriff attended their church and Beth had questioned him relentlessly on the best choice of car to purchase when Lily had earned her license. Up until then, she had made due with an older model car, but Beth wasn't going to take any chances with Lily's safety. Beth had bought her a newer model car with a five star safety rating.

"Thank, God," Beth whispered, desperately trying to hang on to her control in front of the group of men.

The Sheriff nodded. "Someone was definitely looking out for her."

Loker spoke up. "Was it Ton's fault?"

"No, or Lily's, either. Lily said her brakes went out, that was why she couldn't stop. She pulled out in front of Ton. Beth, I'm going to have the car towed to the station and have our mechanic take a look at the brakes."

"I just had the car serviced last month. I just don't know how something like this could have been possible."

"I'll let you know what we find out as soon as possible."

"Thanks, Sheriff. Can I go in and see Lily?"

"The doctor is waiting to talk to you then he'll show you to Lily's room."

Beth went to go inside the door, but hesitated and turned back to Loker. "I want to see Lily, but I don't want Ton upset. Would you find him and let him know he wasn't responsible, along with the news that Lily will be fine?"

"I'll handle it."

"Bring him in to see Lily. He won't rest until he does," Beth commanded.

"Beth, we won't intrude," Loker protested.

"Bring him back or I will come to get him," Beth threatened.

Loker smiled, finally agreeing. He took her by the arm, stopping her before she could leave. "Beth your first concern should have been for Lily, but instead you took the time to comfort a man that could have been responsible for her death. I never give out markers—I pay my debts—but I'm in your debt. If you ever need anything, let me know."

Beth just shook her head at him and went to find Lily's doctor. She wasn't aware of the incredulity on the faces of the men around her. She was the first person, man or woman, to hold a marker for the head of The Last Riders.

CHAPTER SEVEN

Beth signed the last paper, releasing her sister. "Are you ready?"

Lily nodded then winced at the action. Seeing Beth's worried frown, she hastily spoke, "I'm fine. I just have to remember to keep my head still."

Beth touched Lily's pale face. "Let's go home. Evie was supposed to meet us outside twenty minutes ago."

The orderly pushed Lily in a wheelchair to the hospital entrance with Beth following behind, carrying Lily's overnight bag. Once outside, Beth searched the parking lot for Evie's car, but didn't see it. She was about to reach inside her purse for her cell phone when a dark blue car pulled up in front of them.

When Razer and Shade both got out of the car, Beth could only stare in stunned surprised while Razer opened the back door with a smile at the openly surprised women.

"Your chariot awaits, ladies," Razer said with a casual smile.

"But Evie is picking us up," Beth protested. She didn't want to get in the close confines of the car with Razer, and Lily was looking even unhappier at the idea.

"Evie was, but Loker called. He rented this car until

yours is repaired. He asked us to drop it off to you."

"He shouldn't have done that. Ton wasn't responsible for the accident."

"You can take that up with him. Loker didn't want to leave Ton alone so he asked me. I wasn't busy, so here I am. Now, are you ladies ready to roll?"

Beth helplessly rolled her eyes at Lily, stepping back as Razer maneuvered the wheelchair away from the orderly. Deftly, he guided the wheelchair to the waiting car. Razer pushed the wheelchair as close as possible then turned to Beth.

"Get in on the other side and help her slide in." Beth hesitated, though she knew she had little choice.

Going to the other side of the car, she opened the door. Once inside, she helped Lily into the car, carefully adjusting her sprained ankle. As Lily's scared eyes met hers, Beth gave her a reassuring smile.

"You good?" Shade had bent down next to Lily to ask.

"Yes." Her response was tremulous as her hand reached down to smooth down the dress that had ridden up her slim thighs. When Shade's eyes followed her movement, Beth realized he wasn't wearing his sunglasses. His baby blues should be illegal without the sunglasses hiding them. Beth thought any young girl, faced with a specimen such as Shade, would use the opportunity to flirt outrageously, yet Lily leaned away and averted her face. Beth didn't know whether to be concerned or thankful.

Razer shut Beth's door before getting into the front seat while Shade closed Lily's door, also getting into the front.

The ride was quiet for a few minutes before Razer filled the taut silence with innocuous comments on the rental car. The conversation relaxed the girls, their stiffened bodies gradually sinking into the luxurious seats. The conversation steadily switched to how Lily was enjoying college. Her responses were at first stilted, but as she talked about her classes, she became more animated until she almost seemed relaxed by the time they pulled up in front of Beth's house.

Razer went to the trunk to get Lily's overnight bag and crutches after he opened Beth's door while Shade waited next to an already opened door by Lily, moving away when Beth took the crutches from Razer. She helped Lily from the car and the trio watched as the girl put the crutches under her arms, wincing when she lifted them.

"I guess I'm still a little stiff." Lily tried to laugh it off.

With the crutches under her arms, she took a step forward slowly with a small whimper escaping from her pursed lips, yet she didn't stop attempting another step. Her discomfort was obvious to the onlookers; they all could see she was in extreme pain.

"For Christ's sake," Shade finally exploded and then lifted a startled Lily into his arms without warning. The crutches fell to the ground and Lily's body arched as she tried to throw herself out of his arms.

Beth started to go to her, but Razer took her by the arm, leading her to the house.

"Wait, I can walk on the crutches." Desperately, Lily tried to wrench out of his arms. Shade gave her a small toss into the air, which automatically caused Lily's arms to circle his neck, holding on to him.

"Be careful, you don't want me to drop you." Shade laughed, walking to the door of the house. Lily loosened her grip on his so that she could lean back without being pressed so close to his chest while also giving herself more breathing room.

As he brought Lily into the house, Beth and Razer were waiting inside. "Where do you want her?"

Beth motioned to the couch, which had been purchased for visiting members of the church and was already pulled out into a bed, ready for Lily's use. Beth didn't want to confine Lily to the upstairs with her foot.

Shade gently laid Lily on the bed, making sure she was comfortable before leaving without a word.

Speechless, Beth simply stared at the closed door. "Yes… well… thanks for picking us up." Beth turned as the door opened again to see Shade carrying the crutches. He leaned them against the couch, close to Lily and, again, left without a word.

"Shade's not big on manners," Razor tried to excuse his friend while fighting his own amusement as the women merely gaped at him.

"Is he going to come back again?" Beth asked, staring at the door.

"No, I think that was it for now. Is there anything I can do for you before I leave?" Both women shook their heads.

"All right. Then I'll catch you later." Razer went to stand next to Lily, touching her bandaged forehead. "Stay safe."

"Thanks." Lily shyly smiled at Razer who then, not about to let Shade outdo him, left without another word.

As soon as the door closed with a snap, the sisters gawked at each other. They both couldn't help wondering why the men had been so considerate and helpful when it was such a contradiction to the tough biker image they normally projected.

CHAPTER EIGHT

Dean called Beth several times throughout the week to check in on Lily, but anytime the conversation became personal, he would switch topics. Beth hung up from their latest conversation confused at his strange behavior. He had yet to become amorous towards her after months of dating, although he had definitely led her to believe that they were headed that way. She had thought the trip to Las Vegas would bring a new level of intimacy to their relationship. Now Dean was acting once again like her Pastor. Beth didn't know what to make of it. Lily was going back to school tomorrow and Beth would be driving her. She had hoped that he would offer to keep her company, instead he had mentioned a scheduled meeting with a parishioner.

* * *

Early the next day, the sisters left Treepoint while it was still dark; it was a three-hour drive so they decided to stop and eat breakfast before driving on to Lily's dorm. The college was bustling with students outside the large dorm by the time they pulled up. Beth walked by Lily's side as they passed through the common room to reach the elevators, noticing that none of the other students said hi or even acknowledged Lily.

"Have you made many friends, Lily?"

Lily paused in opening her door before answering truthfully as she entered her room.

"Not really. I guess I thought that because it was a religious college, the other students would be serious about their courses. They think because I don't go to their get-togethers that I don't want to be friends."

Beth hugged her sister, remembering how uncomfortable she had felt her freshman year.

"It'll get easier. You will find students you have more in common with, don't get discouraged."

"I won't. It doesn't bother me, I need to study more than I need friends to distract me."

"I'm sure your studies won't suffer if you take time to go out for lunch or dinner. Don't close yourself off to new acquaintances or experiences."

Lilly grinned. "I won't."

Beth left her sister sitting at her small desk, pulling books out of her backpack. She worried about how isolated Lily seemed on the lonely drive home. It was late afternoon when she arrived back in Treepoint and pulled into the Sheriff's Office. He had called yesterday to ask her to stop by his office, so she had promised to stop in on her way back from dropping Lily off.

The receptionist showed her to his office immediately. As she walked towards the office she couldn't help thinking of the history between the sheriff and her family. Will Hunter had been sheriff for the last fourteen years and had attended her father's church. There wasn't much he didn't know about the small community and what he didn't, he made it his mission to find out. If it could adversely affect the town he protected, every measure was taken to see that the townspeople remained safe. Inside and outside the legalities of the law; every recourse at his disposal was used with ruthless disregard. Her father and Will had a tumultuous relationship because of this. Beth had often thought that he'd only attended her father's church to keep a cautious eye on the influential church leader.

"Hello, Beth, have a seat." He rose as she entered the room and then resumed his seat as she took the chair in front of his desk. "Lily doing well?" The sheriff picked up an ink pen lying on his desk, sliding it back and forth between his fingers.

"Yes, still a little sore, but she's much better. Thank you for asking. You said you had some news on my car?"

The pen was put back on the desk as he clasped his hands together, leaning towards Beth. "Yes, I am afraid you're not going to like what the report confirmed, either. The mechanic found your brake lines had been tampered with; someone definitely wanted to hurt, if not kill you. Everyone in town knows you're constantly driving up and down those mountain roads, which are treacherous on a good day with a car in good working order. They'd be deadly in a car with no brakes."

Concerned, Beth sat forward in her chair. "You are sure Lily wasn't the intended victim?"

The sheriff leaned back in his seat, shaking his head. "No, Lily drives the car too infrequently. When someone wants someone dead, they pick a plan that has the highest chance of success at the first attempt. Do you have any ideas as to who would want to hurt you? Anyone you made angry lately? Old boyfriends?"

Beth could only shake her head negatively to each question.

"All right, think about it and let me know. Be careful, Beth. I've already told my deputies to keep an around the clock check on your house, but you need to be extremely cautious."

"I will Sheriff and, if I think of anyone, I'll call you immediately."

"Don't hesitate to call me day or night."

"When can I get my car back?"

"As soon as you can get someone to come and get it from the lot out back. With the accident and the brakes being tampered with, the insurance company should find it's totaled. I suggest you look for a new car."

Beth left the sheriff's office worried and more than a little frightened. She had not been able to think of a single person who could have a reason to harm her. It wasn't like she led an exciting life; her work and personal lives were extremely tame and she didn't she'd done anything that would give anyone a reason to wish her injury.

Looking at her watch, Beth walked across the street to meet Dean for their weekly dinner date. They had been meeting at the diner every Thursday evening for dinner since they had begun dating.

The diner was never busy during the weeknights and they could enjoy a quiet conversation after work. Finding an empty booth was easy, which was why they had picked the diner; that and because the church was beside the sheriff's office just across the street. It made it convenient when he worked late. Beth had ordered a drink and was scrolling down through the messages on her cell phone that had come in while she was in the sheriff's office when Razer slid into the seat in front of her.

"What are you doing? I'm waiting for someone," Beth said.

"Pastor Dean, I know. When you didn't respond to his message, he didn't want you to be left waiting for him." Glancing at her cell phone, Beth finished reading the message from Dean.

"Since when does Dean use you to pass on his messages?"

"I guess I'm just lucky. I was in the right place at the right time. I offered to relay his message and he took me up on it. Now what are we ordering?"

"Nothing. I'm going home." Beth motioned for the waitress.

Razer stopped her. "Come on, Beth. Don't make me

eat alone. Nothing can happen here. Sit and have dinner with me," Razer wheedled.

Unsure, Beth picked up her glass of water and took a sip as the waitress approached, taking their order. Beth raised her brow at the amount of food he ordered.

"What can I say, I'm a growing boy," he said after the waitress walked away.

More like he needs to keep his energy up to perform all the orgies he participates in every night, Beth thought nastily.

"Now, now. I can read that look on your face; those weren't nice thoughts you were thinking. Care to share?"

"I don't know what you mean," Beth said haughtily.

"Come on, I'll pay for your dinner if you tell me what you were just thinking."

"I can pay for my own dinner."

"Chicken."

Angered, she replied, "I bet it does take a lot of food to supply you with enough energy to keep everybody happy."

With a wicked glint in his eyes, he asked, "Just what do you mean by that?"

"Well, you're delivering cars for Loker James and delivering messages for Pastor Dean."

"Oh, I thought you meant me keeping the girls happy," he whispered seductively. "Baby, I can do it all."

"I know you can. I saw that for myself." Beth was done. She again started to get up, but the waitress placing the food down in front off them forestalled her movement.

"Eat, Beth. I'll behave. Please, it was a lame-ass attempt to bring up an embarrassing situation that I think it would be good for us to clear the air about it."

Beth picked up her fork. "I don't think we need to discuss it at all."

Razer followed her cue and started eating. Beth had long since lost her appetite, though, and now desperately wanted the meal to just be over. Unable to eat more than a few bites of food, Beth sat and watched as he demolished his own food then poached her still full plate.

"Want any dessert?" Razer asked when he finished.

"No, thanks." Beth opened her purse, determined to pay her part and beat a hasty retreat.

Razer, seeing her intent, forestalled the attempt. "Beth, I want to apologize for how things went down with us. I can guess it was an extremely embarrassing situation that you found yourself in that night."

Beth looked out the window, unable to meet his eyes.

"I'd like to start over and get to know you. I handled my attraction to you all wrong. If you give me a chance, I can promise this attraction we feel for each other will be worth the effort."

She immediately shook her head. "I am *not* attracted to you."

"You were. Beth, that night on your couch, you wanted me. You weren't comfortable with me, your values kept you from fucking me, but they didn't stop you from coming on my hand. At my clubhouse, you were overwhelmed with things moving so fast and bolted." When Beth would have interrupted, he ignored her. "Still, you invited me in that night and, stupidly, I said no. Later, you came to me knowing you wanted to fuck me and walked into a situation that shocked you."

Beth looked at him, his words bringing back that humiliating night. "Razer, please, I don't want to go over this. You want the air clear. It's clear. You want to be friends. Fine, we're friends. But we are not now or in the future going to be fuck buddies, which I think is what you want from me. You have your choice of those at your club. You don't need me for that. You showed me that night that you have no respect for women."

Angry now, Razer cut her off, "How did I not respect you, Beth? Did I pressure you into doing something you didn't want? Did I rape you? The minute I saw you weren't on the same page as me in my bedroom, I let you leave. Did I call you any names or try to change your mind?"

"No," Beth admitted.

"None of the men in the club disrespect the women there. Yes, we share a highly sexual relationship, I admit. We enjoy each other not only as sexual companions, but we share friendships. None of us want a typical relationship. We are not ashamed of our lifestyle and don't feel the need to explain it to strangers. To enter our club is a choice both the men and the women freely make. Especially the women we do not recruit. The women all seek entrance on their own. None of them are forced to be there; in fact, many of the women have been lower members of the club for years, performing many jobs that benefit the club."

Before Beth could jump in and say "blowjobs", Razer shook his head as if reading her mind. "No; relaying messages, accounting, taking messages, delivering messages and yes, providing sex. If they don't want to stay, they leave, but we have rules for them to become members, to make sure it's the type of life they want. And no one is coercing them into anything they are not comfortable doing."

"I can't handle a man going from woman to woman," Beth stated and then confessed, "Sex has to mean something to me. I know it's old fashioned."

"Not old-fashioned, sweets. Though, Beth, I have to be honest, my dick doesn't have a woman's name on it and it won't ever. I like sex and enjoy a variety of partners. I practice safe sex and the others in the house do, too; it's a hard rule. Anyone caught not doing so leaves the club. On the other hand, I can understand and respect your views on sex. Can't you do the same? I'm not asking you to have sex tonight or introduce you to a threesome," he teased at her shocked expression. "But we could see where this attraction goes, maybe draw closer and have a little fun, or be able to move on with it out of our systems."

He took her hand that was lying on the table and gave it a tight squeeze.

"I've been seeing Pastor Dean."

"I know and I talked to him. He was going to talk to you tonight, but I decided to do it for him."

"You didn't want me talking to him, yet you freely admit to having unlimited sex. You're unbelievable."

"We don't share outside the club. It's a rule," he explained patiently.

"The club rules don't matter to me."

"I hope someday they will." Razer forestalled her sharp reply. "That's an argument for another day. One that, in all probability, will never come. Right now, tonight, I just want us to agree that you'll give me another chance."

Beth sat there, sick to her stomach at the temptation in front of her. She would never be able to handle his lifestyle. The thought of him with other women made her ill. Unlike last time, Beth was smart enough to realize that he was going to be with other women; whether he was with her or not.

Even though they hadn't been together, it hadn't hurt any less over the last nine months. Every night, as she lay in bed with her burning body driving her insane, she knew he was fucking numerous women without a thought of her in his mind. The only consolation she now had was that Razer hadn't been able to forget her, either, or he wouldn't be here.

Beth knew it would be wrong to go to a man of Dean's caliber with her body on fire for another. She made the decision, one that she knew deep in her heart she would regret, but she would not back away from it like a coward. She was going to let Razer into her life.

God help her.

CHAPTER NINE

Beth handed Evie her paycheck.

"I can give you more hours next week if you need them, but it would be only temporary. Mrs. Rogers fell and broke her hip. She wants to hire us for two weeks until her daughter can quit her job and move down here permanently."

"That would be cool. The guys will be out of town for a few weeks. Beats sitting around the house, bored."

Beth didn't respond, instead she began clearing the cluttered paperwork at her desk. She and Evie had been going over the clients' files.

She hadn't mentioned her unexpected dinner last evening with Razer. Beth had told him that she would think about their talk and then decide what was best for them both. He hadn't pressured her for a firm answer. He was seemingly content that at least Beth was considering seeing him again.

"Got plans this weekend?" Evie asked, drawing her mind back into the conversation.

"No, just paperwork that keeps piling up."

"The girls and I are going to party at *Rosie's*. I would really like for you to join us," she ventured hesitantly.

"I really need to get that paperwork done."

"The guys won't be there; they're leaving tonight. Sam won't, either; without the guys, she's not interested. It's my birthday and I would really like you come," Evie pleaded.

Beth knew she couldn't refuse Evie's sincere request. They had become friends over the last few months and she didn't want to seem churlish by refusing.

"Okay, I'll be there. What time?"

"I can pick you up."

"I have to help Mrs. Rogers get settled in at home. She's getting released in the afternoon, but a neighbor will spend the night. I'll take my clothes, get changed there and then drive to the club."

Evie reached out and gave Beth an enthusiastic hug. "We'll have a great time. You'll see."

"I know we will." Laughing at an obviously excited Evie, Beth went to her closet and took a package from the shelf before closing the door, handing it to an obviously surprised Evie.

"You knew it was my birthday tomorrow?"

"Of course, you did give me your personal information for withholding taxes. I remembered the date." Beth shrugged as if it was a simple task to remember such a thing.

"I have been with Knox three years, even though he would deny it, and he never remembers my birthday. No one has remembered my birthday since I was a kid."

"Evie, I didn't mean to make you sad. I wanted to make you happy. Open your present," Beth encouraged, warmed by Evie's reaction to her present.

Evie eagerly opened the present as if savoring the moment. When she lifted the lid, her eyes rose to Beth's before she laid the box down on the table, pulling out the shimmering, silky, jade-green top. When she lifted the top, she discovered the box also contained a pair of onyx bangle bracelets and matching ear studs.

"I don't know what to say," Evie said, overwhelmed.

"Then don't say anything. Enjoy."

* * *

Evie held the silky top in her hands, afraid she would wrinkle it. Tears gathered in her eyes, however the woman who considered herself the toughest bitch among the other women, simply put the top back in the box, carefully gathered her things, and said a hasty goodbye. When Evie closed her car door from within, assured there were no prying eyes, she hit her steering wheel with her closed fists, trying to restore her emotions.

"She is unbelievable," Evie ranted to herself. "She remembers one fucking compliment I paid her nine months ago and she buys me one even prettier. What woman does that? We are jealous bitches. Who buys a fucking gorgeous top for the woman who fucked the guy you're crushing on?"

Evie and Razer had not touched each other since that night. Before then, they'd had sex regularly. Evie had spent many nights sleeping in his bed, too tired after the workout he'd given her to leave since Razer hadn't insisted. Yet, things had changed afterwards.

The look of hurt on Beth's face that night still twisted Evie's gut. She couldn't even think of being with Razer now. The fact that Beth hadn't held it against her, but had given her a job with the hours she requested, saw to it she had insurance, and even paid her more than the going rate of a professional with her. She even took care of Evie with the same love and respect that she showed her sister, Lily.

Looking at the box sitting in the seat next to her, Evie put the car in gear. She was determined, if it was the last thing she did, that she would make amends for the part she had unintentionally played in ripping the veil of innocence from Beth.

There were easier ways to learn a guy was a ho. Hell, it was the house joke that Razer would nail any available breezy. He enjoyed sex and boy, was he good at it. He would play with a woman or women for hours, yet get just as much enjoyment laying back, lazily stroking her breasts while another member fucked her. There wasn't an aspect of sex Razer hadn't tried and he had even managed to invent a few. Beth may have deserved to know this, but she sure didn't deserve to be smacked in the face with the knowledge like she had been.

Evie smiled evilly as she drove home. If she was any judge of character, Beth was Razer's Armageddon. He was about to become, with a little help from her—of course— a reformed man-whore, within reason—of course. Evie didn't want Beth denied all the fun.

* * *

Beth finished putting Mrs. Rogers's dirty laundry in the washing machine and, hearing the soft snores of a heavily medicated patient, she went into the spare bedroom. She had asked permission earlier to shower and dress there before leaving. She showered slowly, not in a big rush to join Evie and her friends at the bar. Planning on making her excuses after a few drinks, Beth was nervous of spending time with them. She didn't have any experience of partying with a group of females and knew she would either put a damper on their good time or provide a form of amusement with her presence.

Checking with Mrs. Rogers one final time, she left.

Her blouse was baby blue and clung to the full curves of her breasts, looking very sexy, while a pink leather jacket hid the fact it was a halter that left the back bare. Her jeans clung to her slim hips, barely covering her butt and she had a tiny flashing diamond glinting in her bellybutton when it was caught by the light. She would never have had the confidence to dress so seductively if she hadn't been told the men were out of town.

She drove to the bar, wishing she had brought a change of clothes, though. However, she had wanted to feel as pretty as the others because she was fully aware that, even without the men around, they would be dressed sexily. Beth hadn't wanted to stick out among them.

She wasn't wrong, either. As she entered the bar, Beth could immediately see that she still was dressed conservatively. The majority of them were in short skirts that left little to the imagination and barely there tops. Their high-heeled shoes looked like they were bought at the sex shop in Lexington, not that Beth had ever been in one.

The booze was already flowing and, when Evie saw Beth, she screamed with delight. "I was beginning to think you weren't going to show."

"I told you I would be here. I wouldn't miss your birthday party," Beth said

"We were going to whip your ass if you disappointed our girl," a red head Beth hadn't been introduced to threatened.

"Have a seat, Beth." Evie pulled out a chair next to her. "Been saving it for you for a while," she reprimanded.

"Sorry."

Evie nodded, already forgiving her boss and friend. "Mick, bring Beth a drink."

"Let me introduce everyone." Evie motioned to the gorgeous women sitting at the table. "That's Jewell, Ember, Stori, Ivy, Tricks and Dawn. They are all members of the club. Bliss and Natasha are both newbies." She motioned at the women approaching the table, carrying trays of drinks. She gave each woman a smile as they were introduced. The last two girls gave her eager smiles. The women were definitely sexy, dressing in clothes that screamed 'do me'. Beth envied them for their sexual confidence.

Bliss smiled in return as she placed an unrecognizable drink in front of Beth.

"What is this?" Beth asked her.

"It's a birthday cake martini."

"Well, that explains the sprinkles."

"We *are* celebrating Evie's birthday," Bliss laughed in response.

"I usually do it with a cake," Beth said, taking a tentative sip.

"Come on, Beth, have fun tonight. Mick's giving everyone rides home tonight with the men gone."

"Don't remind me," Jewell moaned. "I hate it when they go out of town."

"Don't they let you go with them?"

"No. When they go out of town, it's usually on business or to settle a problem. They don't want us involved in that shit, so they leave us home, sitting on our asses," Jewell answered. "Doesn't mean we do without while they are gone. Just not as much fun without balls."

Beth blushed, lifting the strong drink to her lips.

"Ignore them," Evie laughed.

Beth finished her drink slowly, looking around the bar. It was empty save for the women at the table.

"It's not very busy in here for a Saturday night, is it?" Beth questioned.

The women burst out laughing while Beth was left wondering what was so funny. She didn't get the chance to ask, not that she really felt like she had the nerve to, because Jewell and Ivy got up, going to the small dance floor and began dancing with each other. A couple of the others got up to join them and Evie was drawn into a conversation with Bliss and Natasha about the small size of Treepoint.

As she glanced around the bar, Beth noticed two men come in and order drinks. She found herself thinking that one was pretty cute and the other not so bad either, which was when Beth realized she was loosening up. The guys didn't stay long after their one drink, leaving with regretful looks at the boisterous table filled with scantily clad women, and Beth found herself feeling a little deprived by the absence of the eye-candy until Bliss drew Beth's attention.

Bliss was the quietest at the table and, for that reason, she felt a sort of kinship with her. Short, spiky blond hair with a lithe, tanned body, Bliss was the woman that she had seen Knox with at the house. Natasha, with her long, curly, brown hair and curves in all the areas that men would find hard to resist, seemed to have made friends with the other girls faster than Bliss.

"How long have you been in Treepoint?" Beth asked Natasha when she was caught staring.

"A year."

"How did you end up here?"

"My cousin is a member of the club's Ohio headquarters. I would visit her on vacations. Met Train and Rider, so I decided to follow them up here. I don't know if I'll be staying here once I am a member, though. No offense, but it's a small town."

"None taken. That's why many of the younger population are leaving. No malls and, other than the movies, not much to keep you busy."

The women burst out laughing. "We stay pretty busy."

"Shut up," Evie said. "Beth is going to think all we do is party all day. We don't."

"No, mainly catch up on the sleep they don't let us get the night before." The girls laughed even harder.

Evie threw the women nasty looks. "I agree a few of you have been shirking your duties, but when Viper gets here, that shit will stop." The laughter immediately stopped and a couple of the girls averted their eyes from Evie's.

"Who's Viper?"

"He's the leader. Word around the club is that he's finally going to make his presence known. Shit is about to go down!"

"Better be quiet, Natasha. You haven't been brought in yet and, if they find out your yap is spreading information outside the club, you won't get enough votes to become a member."

Natasha shrugged. "Only need two more."

"How many votes does it take to become a member?"

"Six. Got the first two the first week, the next within the last six months. They make sure to spread the votes out to make sure you deserve their trust and you're into the club life."

"That's nice the first two liked you well enough to give you their vote so fast," Beth said innocently.

"Yeah, Knox and Rider always like to fuck the new girls first. They know if the girls can handle them, they're up for anything," Evie said without expression.

Beth didn't want to know how many votes Bliss had acquired so far. Beth looked at Evie, wondering how she handled Knox messing around with the women at the table, even managing to become friends. How could she not resent new women being brought into the club?

"So, to become a member you have to have sex with six of the members?"

Natasha shook her head. "Not any six. If that was the case, I would have been a member months ago. No, you have to fuck a particular six. There are eight men that are the original members that began the club; you have to get six of those eight, or you can't be a member. You can hang around and get laid as much as you want, but you can't know shit about the club. After I get my last vote, I can get my tattoo," she said as if it was a sought after trophy.

"Tattoo?

"Yes." Natasha pointed at the other women's tattoos. Each, from what Beth could tell, was the club emblem with a date. Each date was different, placed on various parts of the body, but Beth noticed most were placed on the curve of their breasts.

"It's the date we got the last vote."

Beth literally wanted to be sick. How could these women be so brazen about something that seemed so sexist to her?

Evie looked directly into Beth's eyes. "Don't misunderstand, Beth. No one here, or the other women at the house, are forced to do anything they don't want."

"Hell, no!" the other's chimed in their agreement.

"The men don't go looking for women to lure in or bring in. All of them seek a way in, either from an acquaintance in the club, or requesting it from a member. They all want the freedom and excitement of belonging to the club. They don't do young. Look around the table, we are all well over the age of twenty-one, know what we like sexually and get it as much as we want it. If we don't, they leave us the hell alone, but the sex with the heads of the club is about trust. Trust that the new member being brought in is loyal to the club, the whole club. You find out a lot about a person when you have sex with them."

"Yeah, it's also hard to betray a person whose cock is your best friend," Jewell snickered.

"Who are the original members?" Beth knew she didn't want to know the answer, yet at the same time, she wanted her worst fear confirmed.

"I shouldn't tell you this. It's none of your business, and I hope you won't repeat it to anyone. Knox and Rider, as you've already been told. Viper as the leader, you could figure out, but I will tell you, Razer is one," Evie said regretfully, aware the knowledge would sting. "To keep you from wondering, neither Bliss nor Natasha have Razer's vote. Yet."

Beth forced herself to remain expressionless. Razer had fucked most of the women at the table; in fact, the only two who he hadn't were Natasha and Bliss. Beth looked at Bliss, finally, not able to keep herself from wondering how many votes she had acquired.

As if reading her mind, Bliss said, "I only have two votes. I haven't been here long." This meant she was eager for additional votes, one of which was Razer's.

"Well, good-luck." Beth didn't know what else to say, so she turned to Natasha, repeating her words.

"Thanks. I'm hoping they won't make me wait long. I've been around the club for a couple years because of my cousin. They respected my cousin who wanted me to wait until I was older. When I turned twenty-one, she gave the go ahead," Natasha replied.

Confused, Beth questioned, "But Sam isn't twenty-one?"

"No, she's not. She's twenty, but she doesn't care if she's a member. She just wants the cock. The men didn't have anything to do with her for a long time. Sam became friendly with Ivy when we went to town and Ivy invited her to one of our parties. Sam ditched her as soon as she got her foot in the door, though," Evie answered her question while Ivy sat quietly, staring into her drink. Beth could tell from the vibes the other girls were putting out that the women didn't like Sam.

"Not to put another woman down, but she was all over the guys from day one. Jeez, she can't keep her hands out of their pants." Beth knew she was telling the truth. Sam had already cut a swatch through the men in town before the bikers had shown up in Treepoint.

"Let's quit talking about that bitch and dance. She'll ruin my mood." Evie grabbed Beth's hand. "Dance with me."

Beth found herself dragged onto the floor with the rest of the women following. The bar remained empty except for the women as they danced, laughing. Mick wasn't even paying attention to them; he was watching a game on the overhead television while the waitress was stocking the bar.

As the girls moved and gyrated to the music, Beth just felt ridiculous standing on the lighted floor, moving back and forth on her feet. She had never learned to dance the way they moved. She was about to find an excuse to go back to the table when the door opened and she froze in place.

The men from the club filed into the bar, swamping it with their boisterous voices and the women on the floor squealed in joy. Several of the girls left to latch on to a member. Evie just kept dancing with Beth as if nothing had happened.

"I thought you said no men."

"Didn't know until this afternoon. I knew, if you found out, you wouldn't come and I really wanted you to come. Don't be mad."

"I am going to fire you."

"No, you're not, because then you would have to take care of Errol. You hate doing that, I don't. We're a team now."

The sneaky woman was right, but Beth wasn't going to let her off the hook that easily. She was about to give her hell, however a hand sliding across her stomach, pulling her backwards against a swaying body, stopped her.

"Can I cut in?"

"Please do before she busts my ass." With a wave of her fingers, Evie went back to the table, now with several men keeping it warm.

"Miss me?"

"No."

"I missed you." Razer buried his face in her neck, pulling her closer to his hips. Beth could feel the thickening cock in his pants pressed against her ass, making her nervous and excited all in one breath.

"I want to go back to the table."

"Later."

"But—"

"I want to dance with you for a while. Then, I'll get us both a drink."

Razer was seductive, moving his body against hers, guiding her sinuously against his as the others danced around them. His thigh slid between hers, moving back and forth against the crotch of her jeans. Beth wanted to push away from him, but couldn't find the willpower. A small moan escaped her lips as he began to rub faster when the music changed to a quicker beat. His hand on her stomach slid under her top, coming to a rest underneath her breast. His thumb reached up to stroke the curve of her there and then sanity returned to Beth with a rush.

The reminder of his position within the club, as well as his sexual involvement with the women, repulsed Beth. His participation as an original member could not be forgotten and she felt disgust for herself because she was still attracted to him.

Jerking away from his touch, Beth was determined to go back to the table, get her keys and leave.

Razer didn't let her run, though. "Let's get that drink."

Taking her arm, he pulled her to the bar counter where he sat on one of the tall stools then maneuvered Beth to stand between his legs. He swiveled the stool seat so that Beth was effectively trapped between him and the counter. She tried to struggle away.

"Not tonight, Beth. You know it all now. I'm not hiding anything from you. Be brave and hang for a while. I know this blows your little, protected world to smithereens and the only sexual position you have probably tried is missionary." Razer laughed at her angry face. "But, Beth, there is a whole world out there for you to experience."

"Don't laugh at me." Furious with his amusement at her expense, she pushed at the hard thigh blocking her escape. "You man-whore."

Razer threw his head back, laughing. "Do you think you're insulting me?" He shrugged. "I enjoy sex. In fact, I love sex." He leaned towards Beth, his lips finding her slim throat as his hands grasped her sides, easily lifting her onto her toes until her breasts brushed his chest. "Not everyone believes that sex has to be taken so seriously. It can be fun, sexy, dirty, challenging, and oh so delicious." His tongue slowly licked a path to her ear and then gave a nip on her earlobe.

He was no longer toning down his sexuality with her. He was guns blazing, attempting to seduce her. He was certain that Evie and the other women would have filled her in on all the aspects of the club by now. He'd told

Beth that he would not be faithful to her while they saw each other, so now his conscious was at rest and he was going to try to get her in bed.

"Do you think this makes you desirable to me, Razer?"

"No." Suddenly serious, he leaned back. "Only a certain type of woman is attracted to the type of men in the club. You definitely are not one of them. I thought you were at first and that was why you were attracted to me. I believed you wanted me to work for your pussy, so you pretended to be skittish."

Picking up his drink, he swallowed it in one, quick swallow. Beth lowered her eyes so that he couldn't see her hurt expression. She wanted to stomp out of the bar, her pride intact because of the way he angered and frustrated her with his attitude toward everything. He was her direct opposite.

Suddenly, she finally understood his attraction for her. Opposites attract was an old saying, but in their case, it was true. They were complete, polar opposites. As uptight and morally repressed as she was, Razer was lighthearted and experienced. Her father had stifled her until all his convictions and rules had become normal. Her sexuality had become so repressed it had tried to escape, which was her first attempt at an affair with Razer; however, when it became too much for her fledgling sexuality, she had attempted to cut and run.

Beth had a decision to make. She knew she could never, nor did she want to, develop a laissez-faire attitude towards sex, but she could have fun. Maybe she would even allow herself to experience another mind-blowing orgasm from Razer. She simply had to be smart, take a card from the other women and not let her heart become attached.

Determined, Beth let her hand reach out and lay on Razer's thighs.

"I would like a drink."

Razer narrowly managed to keep from spitting out his

new drink, shocked at the tone in her voice. "Mick, give Beth a drink."

Beth heard Mick set the bottle on the counter behind her, yet she was too embarrassed to face him. She had let her weight relax against Razer, while he let his hand move to her back, sliding down to her ass as he pulled her even closer. Her body pressed tightly against him, her mound resting against his covered cock.

Razer didn't care why she had given in. He had been given his fantasy; her relaxed against him, pliant and wanting. The desire between them simmered as they talked quietly. Other members, both male and female, would join the conservation occasionally as they ordered drinks from the bar. As Beth listened to them talk on a variety of topics, she was able to get to know each of them personally.

When a crowd began forming, Razer stood and moved them to a table at the back of the bar, pulling her down onto his lap. Beth didn't demur as he again became a focal point. Knox and Evie had followed them over, taking chairs across the table that faced Beth and Razer while Rider took the chair beside Razer. Evie and Beth talked casually about driving to Lexington one weekend to shop at the mall and also going to a medical supply store to pick up some items to make their clients' lives easier.

Part of the way through their conversation, Knox slid his hand between Evie's thighs. "You get me hard when you talk nurse."

Evie attempted to pull his hand away, looking at Beth's embarrassed reaction. "She's my boss, you idiot."

"Not here, not tonight. When you're on her dime, she can judge. Right now, I want to watch you come. I think she can handle it. What do you think Razer?"

Razer laughed. "I think so. I'll see what I can do to distract her."

"I would appreciate it." Knox's voice was thick.

He nuzzled Evie's top away from her braless breasts,

taking the tight nipple in his mouth. Beth watched, unable to stop as Evie was pulled onto Knox's lap. Beth's attention was solely focused on the couple making out across from her until it was redirected as Razer's hand, which had casually been resting on her thighs, slid up to her pussy, roughly stroking her through her jeans. When she would have jumped up from his lap, Razer used the opportunity to open her thighs, getting a firmer hold while his other hand gripped her breast and held her in place on his lap. His fingers sought and found the hard nipple hiding behind her thin bra, playing with it ruthlessly. Beth instantly spasmed as she began to feel herself get wet. He lowered his mouth to her neck, sucking gently on a small amount of flesh in the highly sensitive area. Beth felt swamped with desire. She wanted to stop him, but the feeling he was raising in her were an exquisite ache that cried for relief.

Beth could only stare helplessly across the table as Knox unbuttoned Evie's top, baring her pert breasts before putting his mouth on one. Razer unzipped Beth's jeans, his hand sliding inside beneath her panties.

"Wait." Beth pulled furiously at his wrist, looking around to see that no one was paying attention to their table in the darkened corner. Rider, seeing she was conscious of the others in the room, turned his chair until his back blocked the side view of the room.

"Shh... they can't see anything, you're still covered. Knox is blocking the view from the rest of the bar and the only thing they," he nodded toward Knox and Evie, "can see is my hand working you along with the reaction on your face showing you're loving what I'm doing to that wet pussy." She could see that he was right; with Knox blocking the frontal view, Rider on their side and the wall to their left and back, they were enclosed in their own private world. When he felt her relax back into him, Razer's finger entered her tight cunt while his palm worked her clit.

Knox released Evie's breast, raising his lips to her ear to whisper something Beth couldn't hear.

"What did Knox say to you, Evie?" Razer asked. Knox grinned at Razer before he sucked Evie's breast back into his voracious mouth.

"He said…" she stuttered as Knox's hand obviously began rubbing Evie faster.

"Tell him," Knox ordered.

"He said that, when you make Beth come, he wants to watch and then he was… was going to take me out back to fuck me."

"And how am I going to fuck you?" Knox questioned.

"You're going to fuck me hard."

Evie and Beth stared at each other as the men tormented them. Beth watched her friend get manipulated into an orgasm in front of her and was unable to fight the arousal that was burning between her own thighs. Razer slid another finger deep within her and Beth had to bite her lip so she wouldn't scream and draw attention to the table. Her body began to tremble as Razer's hand released the button to the halter behind Beth's neck. When the top slid forward, she reached out to catch the material, but her hand was caught and placed on Rider's jean covered cock instead. He squeezed her fingers tightly against him.

"I can understand why Razer wants you so bad. I am about to come in my jeans watching him fuck you with nothing except his fingers," Rider groaned.

Beth knew she should be shocked by his words, yet she became even wetter as she squirmed on Razer's lap, trying to find release. Curiously, her fingers traced Rider's cock through the jeans, watching as he unsnapped them and let his large cock spring out into her hand. Rider guided her hand over his cock, showing her how he liked it. The shame she knew she should be feeling because she was rubbing one man's dick while another thrust his fingers in and out of her, never came. She was pent up with nothing other than desire.

Watching Evie get worked by Knox while Razer played with her own pussy, Beth's inhibitions lowered until the most important thing was to find a release to the escalating passion. She moved her hand on Rider. She wasn't entirely sure why, she only knew that she wanted to watch him come. As he began thrusting his hips upward, she instinctively knew he was nearing release. She felt like she was being overcome by sensation as Evie's moans drew her attention from Rider and over to where Knox held her tightly in his arms as she orgasmed. Rider's semen filled her hand immediately after and that was the thing that threw Beth into her own climax. Knox practically bounced in his chair as he waited until Rider and Beth were covered before jerking a satisfied Evie out of her chair, hustling her to the back of the bar.

"Want another drink?" Razer asked.

"I think I've had enough."

"You've only had two. Besides, you've only taken a couple sips out of the second."

There went blaming the alcohol for her behavior. Rider and Razer resumed talking as if nothing had happened, but Beth was unable to meet their eyes, she was mortified at her behavior for losing control and actually touching two men at the same time while other's watched.

Later, Knox and Evie returned, yet Beth was too embarrassed to meet her eyes also. Razer, seeing what was going on, frowned at her.

"You're making Evie feel bad. Stop it."

True to his word, Beth saw Evie was becoming upset and wasn't trying to hide it. It was a rare thing to see Evie emotional. She didn't seem to let anything ever touch her, so Beth knew she must be truly embarrassed about her part in the earlier situation.

Beth got up and hugged her friend. "I'm sorry. I didn't mean to make you feel uncomfortable. I was only embarrassed about my part in it. I have never done anything like that in my life." Beth was conscious of the others at the table listening, but wanted to reassure her friend.

"Really, Beth, that was tame considering some of the things we do."

"I can only guess," Beth said wryly.

Conversation returned to normal after that. Evie and Beth talked about work while the guys had their own conversation going. At twelve, Beth rose, excusing herself to everyone at the table.

"I need to get home. I have to relieve Mrs. Roger's neighbor in the morning." Razer nodded, handing Beth her purse and pink jacket. Saying goodnight, Beth left with Razer following.

On the walk to the car, the fresh air felt good on Beth's face as Razer reached out, pulling her to his side and wrapping an arm around her shoulders. They didn't speak; they simply walked together in a comfortable silence. When they got to her car, Beth bent slightly to put the key into the lock and heard a loud popping noise. The next thing she knew, Razer was shoving her into the now open car.

"Stay down," Razer yelled before slamming the door quickly, jerking his phone out of his jean pocket. Someone inside the bar must have heard the shot because the club members came out, each calling out to see what had happened.

Razer signaled them to silence, taking off toward the location the shot had come from with Rider at his side and Knox following close behind. Beth tried to rise up to see what was happening outside, but Shade had come from behind the bar, positioning himself beside her car door.

"Stay down!" Shade's sharp voice had her instantly lowering herself back down.

Several minutes later, Razer and Knox returned. "Did you find anything?" Shade questioned as they approached.

"No. Rider is still looking."

"Who the fuck would be brave enough to piss Viper

off by taking a hit out on you?"

"Don't know."

"Cops here." They watched as the police car pulled into the lot with its lights flashing. Razer opened the car door and Beth hesitantly stepped back out onto the parking lot.

"Who called the police?" Beth asked shakily.

"I did," Razer answered. "Didn't want them thinking we were the ones out here with a gun."

"Beth, Razer." Nodding to the other men, sheriff asked, "What happened?" He didn't beat around the bush.

"Beth and I were by her car when someone fired a shot at me," Razer began explaining.

"Don't expect it was you they were shooting at," the sheriff corrected with a look towards Beth.

"What do you mean?"

"I thought I told you to be careful?"

"I was, but how was I supposed to know someone would be crazy enough to shoot at me in front of witnesses?"

"Someone is trying to kill Beth? Why?" Razer asked, clearly confused.

"I'm still investigating."

"You're investigating? Since when?"

"Since I discovered her car's brakes had been tampered with. I haven't been able to find any prints or witnesses to the tampering. I have the deputies keeping an eye on her. She was supposed to be home like she usually is when she's not working. Someone either had to follow her here or knew she was going to be here. Did you notice anyone following?"

"No, but I wasn't paying attention."

"Show me where the shot came from, Razer. Beth, get back in the car." Beth followed the sheriff's order and got back in her car. Again, Shade waited until both men returned. Beth sat inside the car, watching the men talk. Finally, with a wave, the Sherriff walked back to his car.

Beth's car door was then opened by a very stern

looking Razer. "Slide over."

"What?"

"Slide over, I'm driving."

Beth slid over as Razer took her place behind the wheel. "I can drive myself home."

"You're not going home." Razer made a left onto the road. Beth had a terrible feeling she knew where he was taking her.

"I am not going to your home."

"Yes, you are. Treepoint is incredibly small. Anyone trying to hurt you will be aware of every move you make. The only safe place for you is my place."

"I can stay with Mrs. Rogers; no one would know I was there."

"What if you're wrong? Do you want to take a chance on getting her hurt?"

"No."

"Then you agree."

CHAPTER TEN

The huge house looked the same as it had the last time she was there.

"I don't think I can do this." Beth tried to pull her hand out of Razer's as they walked up the steps to the opened front door.

"Beth, I don't think you understand. I'm not giving you a choice." Razer stood grimly by the door as she walked inside. Evie and the rest of the club members had been waiting in the living room for them to arrive. They had left the club while the sheriff and Razer were talking.

"Are you all right?" A worried Evie asked as soon as she saw Beth's white face.

"Yes, just surprised someone wants me dead. It's not like I'm a member of a motorcycle club or something," Beth joked. Razer laughed, lightening the mood of the room.

"Yeah, that's why. When we were shot at, I assumed the shot was aimed at me." Razer liked that she had a sense of humor when most women would have been frightened at the situation Beth found herself in.

Everyone in the group laughed, except Evie. "Don't joke. It's not a laughing matter."

"No, it's not," Razer said in agreement. "But it's good that Beth can keep a handle on it and remain calm."

"I just can't understand why someone would try to murder me."

"Whatever the reason, they almost accomplished their goal. If you hadn't bent when you had, they would have had a head shot. Evie, Beth is supposed to be at Mrs. Rogers in the morning, can you fill in for her?"

"Of course."

"That's not necessary," Beth protested.

"Yes, it is. You can't go to church tomorrow, either. Your schedule has to be completely random. Each day it will be different; the lengths of time sporadic."

"Don't worry, I can handle the work. Remember, I told you earlier that I wanted the extra hours."

"But that was when you thought the guys were still going out of town."

"It doesn't matter. When this is over, give me a few days off."

Beth yawned.

"Let's go to bed." Razer and Beth left as the others also began heading upstairs.

Beth felt a little guilty that Evie's birthday celebration had been brought to an end by the mysterious shooter as she wearily climbed the stairs, sleepily wondering whose room she would be borrowing for the night. When Razer opened the door to his room, she was surprised to see that it was tidy with the bed neatly made.

"I appreciate you giving up your room for the night—" Beth began, only to see him taking his shirt off and throwing it on the chair beside the bed.

"What are you doing?"

"Getting ready for bed. The bathroom is through that door." He opened a drawer of the huge chest against the wall, pulling out a white t-shirt and handing it to her.

"I am not sleeping in your bed with you." Scandalized, Beth went to leave the room.

"Are you for real?" Razer snapped.

"Don't be an ass. I am not sleeping with you."

"Yes. You. Are. No one gives up their room here. All the bedrooms are spoken for, the couch in the living room is full and so are the two in the back room. Even if they were available, though, you still wouldn't sleep alone. One of the other men would be on you in a second."

"They would rape me?"

Razer sighed heavily. "No, but you wouldn't sleep alone. Come on, Beth, I won't bother you tonight. Let's get some sleep. I'm tired, too." He did look tired and Beth knew she was acting ridiculous.

"All right." Beth gave in; she really was too tired to argue further.

Beth took the t-shirt and went into the clean bathroom, getting ready for bed. After washing the light make-up from her face, she reluctantly went back into the bedroom where Razer was already in bed. His eyes followed her across the room. Hastily, she slid onto the mattress and pulled the covers up to her chest.

"Need anything?"

"No, thank you." The light went out and Beth laid back stiffly, angry with herself for how silly she was acting.

Razer simply made her so nervous that she didn't know how to react. Her body wanted him, but her mind held her back. Her father's teachings had become so ingrained into her psyche that she automatically fought to reject the desires that burned inside her. The intellectual side of her knew that there was nothing wrong with expressing her sexuality in a committed relationship, yet the true hesitation that held Beth back was that she knew Razer didn't want a committed relationship. He wanted a purely sexual one that left his heart and emotions free to come and go among the other women. Beth couldn't handle that. It would destroy her and Beth refused to leave herself so vulnerable.

When she turned onto her side, closing her eyes, a hard

arm slid around her waist and dragged her into his warm body. Beth didn't protest because it made her feel safe and, as much as she hated to admit it, she was scared. The thought of someone actually feeling enough malice towards her to cause physical harm had her nerves screaming in terror.

Beth had never done confrontations well. She always backed down. Even in school, she had never gotten into an argument. She was an out and out coward and freely admitted it, but she was good at hiding her emotions. No one had figured out she was terrified, not even Razer.

Razer pulled her tighter against him and the terror eased as her body melted against him, content that at least tonight he was hers. As she fell asleep, Razer felt her grip finally loosen on his arm around her waist. He didn't know which had frightened her more, the person trying to kill her or sharing a bed with him. He had lied when he had told her that the men wouldn't let her sleep alone, easily maneuvering her exactly where he'd wanted her. They wouldn't have gone near her unless she'd asked or given an invitation; however, Razer had no intention of telling the timid kitten that little bit of knowledge. Tonight, she was in his bed right where he wanted her.

CHAPTER ELEVEN

Beth woke up with an urgent desire to use the bathroom. Looking out the only window in the room, she saw that it must be early morning. Razer was lying on his stomach with his bare ass peaking out from the blankets. How had she not known he was naked under the covers? Unable to gather her thoughts at the glory before her, she got out of the bed to empty her full bladder.

When she was done and had washed her hands, she turned the light out and went back to bed. Beth was an early riser, but she didn't know what to do with herself if she got out of bed. It wasn't like she knew her way around the house or had work to go to. Her eyes couldn't stay away from Razer and her fingers itched to reach out and touch him. Frustrated with herself, she plumped her pillow and lay back down. As she did, Razer rose and pulled her beneath him.

"Can't sleep?"

"This is the time I usually get up."

"This is the time I'm usually going to bed," he mocked her.

"Yes, but I work." Beth regretted her words at his angry look.

"I work," he snapped.

"You do? I never see you around town."

"That's because I don't work in town, not that there are many jobs available."

"Then what do you do? Do you work online?"

Razer got out of bed and went to the chest, pulling out fresh clothes.

"I'll show you. Get dressed while I take a shower. Evie said she would put some clothes for you outside the door on her way to work."

Beth gathered the clothes sitting neatly outside the door. Evie had picked a pale cream t-shirt and a pair of sweat pants. The shirt was tight, but the pants fit perfect. She was silently grateful to her friend for picking something modest for her. She was combing her hair with the small brush in her purse when Razer walked back in with a towel around his hips.

Beth put the brush down, tugging her hair back into a tight ponytail. She was unable to prevent her eyes from watching Razer drop the towel and get dressed in jeans and a black shirt. Throwing her a smug look, he sat on the side of his bed while putting on his boots.

"Ready?"

"Yes."

Beth was curious about what he was going to show her as she followed him from the room. He led them down the stairs and out the front door. Expecting him to go to his bike, she was surprised when he led them to the factory that had never been opened instead.

He took a key out of his pocket and unlocked the door. Lights came on, flooding the huge area. She wasn't sure what she would find, but stacks of boxes and merchandise was not one of her guesses.

"We actually work in the warehouse. Each of us works various shifts. A morning or afternoon shift, four days a week. We close Friday thru Sunday."

"What do you make?" Beth was impressed.

"Several items." He walked to one table with several packaged boxes waiting to be shipped. He picked one up, handing it to her. As she looked it over she could see it was a survival kit. "I'm a chemical engineer. My job is to find ways to keep food from spoiling and to make foods that previously were unable to be preserved, preservable." Walking to another table, he picked up another package. Inside it had a plain brown stick and the box said it was able to draw energy from the environment. "Shade is a mechanical engineer, Evie decides what goes into the medical kits, Knox is our computer engineer and develops our programs so that our customers can order online. You name it, one of our people are experienced in that field."

"You guys supply the Doomsdayers."

Razer laughed. "Yes, but not only them. Countries that have a high probability for natural disasters order them to keep their families safe. Our customers are from a wide variety of demographics."

"You guys are a corporation?"

"Yes, all the full members living in the house are stockholders, some with a larger piece than the others. Except for Natasha and Bliss. When they become full members, they'll be given a share."

"I can't believe this. I had no idea. No one in town does. They believe you're a motorcycle gang that steals and sells drugs."

"You can't tell anyone, Beth. It goes against the rules for me to show this to you."

"Then why show it to me?"

"Because I didn't want you thinking I was too lazy to work for a living. I also didn't want you thinking the club was guilty of illegal activity. If you thought that, why go out with me?"

"I said people in town thought that, not that I did. I never believe gossip." She walked around the factory, asking questions when it was a product she had never seen before or used in a different way than its intended use. He showed her a small lightweight shovel that had ten different uses, one as a deadly weapon. She was going to order one for herself.

"I wish you had involved the community more; jobs are needed desperately."

"That was our plan, in the beginning, until our money was stolen."

It finally clicked with Beth. "Your corporation put up the original money for the plant. You own the factory, plant and land around here."

"The six of us on the board were in the military together and came up with this idea. We pooled every dime we had together and what we could borrow from our families. Everything was on track to open when the machinery was ordered and then the money to pay for it vanished."

Beth nodded. "Gavin Stolmes took it and disappeared."

"No, Gavin's older brother is the club leader. Viper sent him to Treepoint to handle everything up here while we worked in Ohio. We worked hard and put all our cash into opening this factory. He didn't steal the money from his own brother and the club, he was murdered. We can't prove it, his body has never been recovered, but we know that's what happened. Until we find out who killed Gavin, we won't open the factory to outsiders."

Beth nodded her understanding. "I don't think you'll ever discover who murdered him, though. Whoever did it obviously covered their tracks well. The people here love to gossip about everyone's dirty little secrets, but anything criminal that could potentially harm their families, you'll find their mouths zipped shut."

"That's what we discovered. That's why we let Sam hang out; we were trying to find out what we could about the locals."

"I don't think that's the only reason Sam hangs out. Does she know about this?"

"No, we keep her away. She's not allowed on the property Monday through Thursday."

"Perhaps I could ask around and see what I could find out."

"Don't even think about it. You already have a big enough target on your back."

The sound of a car pulling up outside had them looking towards the window which overlooked the parking lot. Evie was parking her car. Beth frowned, she shouldn't have been back so early. Looking at her watch, she discovered they had been in here several hours; it was almost lunchtime.

"Let's go back to the house. You have to be hungry and I am starving."

In the house, voices were coming from the kitchen and, as Beth entered the large room, she found the majority of the members crammed into the kitchen and dining room. Food was set out around the counter as well as a variety of drinks.

Razer handed her a plate, which she filled with eggs, bacon and toast. "We do brunch on Sunday's, usually this would be lunch," Razer explained. He found two spots at the table across from Jewell and Evie. Everyone ate in relative silence and it wasn't until they sat, drinking coffee, that Beth asked about Mrs. Rogers.

"She was fine when I left. Her son showed up with her grandchildren, they were going to stay until the neighbor showed up."

"I'm glad. I felt guilty you working my shift for me."

"Don't be. I'll find a way for you to even the score," Evie joked.

"Anything."

"Careful, Beth. Owing Evie a favor can be a real pain in the ass," Razer warned.

"Shut-up." Evie laughed.

The atmosphere in the room changed when Sam came into the room carrying a cup of coffee.

She sat down next to Knox who was sitting on the other side of Razer. Unlike the other women, who were dressed suggestively in tight jeans and pretty tops, she was clad in a pair of short, boy shorts and a see-through, white tank top. Samantha bypassed suggestive and went straight to fuck me.

"You guys need to fix foods that aren't so fattening. No wonder you're having so much trouble with your weight, Jewell."

Beth's mouth almost dropped open at her catty comment while Jewell simply threw her a dirty look without saying anything. Others finished breakfast and wandered away. Beth heard the sound of dishes being washed and rose to go help. Razer pulled her back down.

"There's a chore list, the house jobs rotate. Evie will put your name on the list and you can take your turn then."

"You do dishes?" Beth couldn't prevent the humor in her voice.

"About twice a month," Razer replied ruefully.

"I brought you some clothes. I went by your house before coming home," Evie told Beth.

"Thank you."

Beth noticed the darkening of Evie's eyes as Sam leaned against Knox, seductively rubbing her breasts against his arm.

"Cut it out, Sam. I'm trying to eat." Knox pulled his arm away.

Sam shrugged, leaning back in her seat. "Shouldn't have given you that blowjob before you came downstairs. Now you don't want to play."

"The problem is you want to play all the time. None of us can keep you satisfied for long," Knox said.

"Oh, I know a couple of members that can hit the right spot the first time. Isn't that right, Razer? Don't suppose you're up for some fun? Little Miss Goody Two Shoes couldn't have gotten you off more than once. I know how you like to go all night." Her hand snaked out to rub his arm on the table.

"Bitch, you better back the hell off!" Evie told Sam, who didn't remove her hand.

Razer pulled his arm away.

"Where are your keys, Evie? I'll get Beth's clothes." Still angry, Evie reached into her pocket and pulled out her keys, handing them to Razer.

"Later." Knox, obviously eager to escape the women's wrath, left with Razer.

With the men gone, Sam was smart enough to know the women weren't going to tolerate her cattiness, so she wisely moved to another table.

"One day, I am going to slap the hell out of her," Evie stated.

"Every woman here wants that honor," Jewell agreed.

Beth sat there listening, her stomach twisting in knots at seeing Samantha's fingers drop to Rider's crotch. She had to find some way out of here before she came face to face with another sexual encounter between Razer and one of the women.

"Beth, she only did that to push our buttons," Evie tried to console her.

"I don't know how you stand to watch men you care about touch other women."

Evie let out a long breath and tried to explain. It was going to be hard to get Beth to understand, but she had to try. "Beth, Sam is a bitch. She does things to get the other women angry. She tries to bring jealousy into our friendships and there are reasons we tolerate her. When the time comes that those reasons no longer exist, her situation will change drastically. Until then, she is an aggravation that you need to ignore, the same as we try to do."

Beth knew that Evie was unaware that Razer had told her about Sam. She should feel glad that no one really wanted Sam around, yet it didn't make her grabbing

Razer's arm any easier to bear.

"Now, I want to address something you said." A blush rose in her cheeks. Beth felt how hard she found it to talk about the subject. "Knox and I are not a couple. I think you are under the misunderstanding that I want a relationship with Knox and he is just using me. We are friends, but those feelings you think are there are not. We enjoy a sexual relationship, although it is one that I also share with other members in the club. You have to understand that your values and morals are not ours and, while we don't criticize your way of life, we would like the same respect. Usually, those among us who have come to care for each other seek housing elsewhere, while still maintaining their membership. It hasn't happened often, but it does happen. We have no couples in the house currently and the members have sex with whom they want. We can be as selective as we want as often as we want, that is the part we enjoy."

"I didn't mean to be judgmental, Evie. Just because a way of life isn't for me, doesn't mean I am not capable of understanding it."

"What makes you think that you wouldn't fit in, Beth?"

Beth blushed bright red. "I know myself."

"I think you would find several aspects of our life very exciting if you would open yourself up to the experience."

Beth shook her head.

"I know how honest you are, Beth. You can't deny what happened last night. Were you aroused watching me with Knox?" Beth didn't say anything, averting her eyes to a spot on the table.

"I know I found it hot as hell watching Razer finger fuck you while you jacked-off Rider. When Knox fucked me against the wall afterwards… whew! I haven't come that hard in a long time." Beth's eyes lifted in shock to Evie, who was giving her a gentle smile.

"I don't know why I liked it," she confessed.

Jewell broke into the conversation. "I do, you were

horny. Girl, you got to relax and get laid."

Beth and Evie both burst out laughing.

"What's so funny?" Razer asked as he walked back into the room.

"Girl talk," Beth said before the two women could say anything more outrageous.

"I put your suitcase in my room. Do you need anything? Shade and I are going to the bar to check out the area where the shot occurred and then ride into town to see if the Sheriff has anything new."

"No, I don't need anything. I think I'll work up a new schedule for Evie and myself."

With orders to Beth to stay inside the house, Razer went in search of Shade. Beth went upstairs alone to catch up on the paperwork Evie had thoughtfully picked up for her. She completed worksheets on the clients, calculated the next week's payroll, and was thinking about organizing Sam's grandmother's files, which were still in the trunk of her rental car, when she became sleepy. Lying down on the bed, she thought she would take a quick cat nap.

Lips at her throat woke her. "Now this is what a man wants waiting for him when he opens his bedroom door." Beth opened her eyes to smile sleepily up at Razer.

"A woman can't go wrong waking to a sexy man." Razer smiled at her reply.

"You think I'm sexy?"

"Yes."

"A man always likes to feel his assets are appreciated."

"Ahh. I'll have to tell you more often then. I don't want you to feel under appreciated."

His lips traced down her chest as his hands tugged the shirt down, exposing her bra-covered breasts.

Beth lay still, letting him explore her body. She was on fire after falling asleep with the memories of last night replaying through her mind. Her defenses were down and she didn't care at that precise moment in time. She wanted the flames burning in her to be extinguished.

Razer turned her slightly towards his body, unsnapped her bra and then pulled both the bra and t-shirt off, throwing them to the floor. He lifted her up to him and sucked a nipple into his mouth. He didn't go easy on her, though he wasn't extremely rough, either. He played with one nipple between his fingers as he teased the other with his mouth.

Moving away, Razer sat up long enough to remove his t-shirt and kick off his boots before lying back down, pulling her back to him.

"You make me want you until my dick hurts, Beth." Beth could only echo his sentiments.

His hands tugged the sweatpants and underwear down her body, tossing them onto the clothes that were already on the floor. Razer's lips covered hers when he saw the realization that her clothes were gone had hit her. His hand went to her pussy where it expertly found her clit, rubbing and teasing her until she writhed beneath him. Her hips actively ground against his hand, trying to increase the pressure instead of the light touches he was using to tease her. One finger slid within her sheathe, moving in and out, which had her whimpering under his mouth, spreading her legs wider in invitation.

"Easy, baby, I don't want you to come yet. My cock is going to be buried in that tight pussy first." His words only heightened her arousal. No one had ever talked dirty to her; it made her feel sexy to hear it coming from Razer.

He squeezed one nipple to a point before sucking the tip into his mouth then slid another finger into her wet pussy. The filling sensation made Beth almost come, but Razer felt her tense and quickly pulled his fingers out and unsnapped his jeans. Sitting back on his haunches, he maneuvered Beth until a leg was on each side of his hips. Reaching sideways, he opened his nightstand drawer, taking out a condom and ripping it open then sliding it onto his hard length.

Beth watched him, not sure if she wanted to finish

what they had started. Her body was ready, but her conscience was holding her back. She wasn't sure she was strong enough to overcome the battle and was about to call a halt when Razer looked at her, reading the indecision on her face.

Instead of becoming angry, Razer felt challenged. "If you're not sure, I must not be doing something right. Do you know how bad I want your little pussy? I wanted you the first time I saw you."

Beth tried to gather her thoughts at his seductive words, however her mind was racing with carnal thoughts now. His hand returned to her pussy where, once again, his fingers began playing.

"You wouldn't remember because you didn't see me." The whole time he talked, his fingers were bringing the urgent need back into her body, making her twist and turn on the rumpled bed. He held her firmly, though, positioning her body exactly where he wanted it. "You were sitting outside the diner with Lily while Shade and I were in the parking lot across the street, getting our bikes inspected. I don't remember what Lily was eating, but you were sitting in the sun, licking an ice cream cone. It reminded me of a kitty lapping up her cream." The images he was drawing in her mind while his thrusting fingers had her arching her hips, creating a frenzy in her where she was unable to stop herself from wanting more of him.

Razer fit his cock against her wet invitation, pressing inward. "I almost came in my jeans that day watching you. Felt like an idiot when the Sheriff handed me the inspection sticker. I hadn't even noticed he was finished." Razer continued his story now as a means to keep himself distracted from coming immediately from the tight warmth sucking him inside. "I knew then that I was going to find a way to get my cock in you." Razer pulled her hips towards him, her silky cunt taking his strokes until he was blocked by a thin piece of skin.

Shocked and more than a little awed, he practically

growled, "Ah… my little kitty is a sweet, little virgin." He gave a hard push of his hips, breaking through the membrane. Beth gave a tiny scream at the pain, but Razer didn't give her time to let it gain control. His hands that had been holding her hips slid down, forming a v, then began stroking her clit, making it peak out. Beth wiggled down further onto his cock, making Razer groan at her movement.

"That's it. My little kitten wants my cock, doesn't she?" Razer rose off his haunches, leaning over Beth, plunging all the way inside her until she felt his tight balls against her ass.

"I am going to let you come now, kitten." Beth frantically nodded her agreement as she continued moving her hips helplessly against his, searching for relief from the orgasm he was ruthlessly guiding her towards. "I'm going to come with you. I'm not going to be too rough, though, because I plan to fuck you all night and you're going to be a good kitty and let me. Okay?"

"Yes… Yes…" Beth agreed.

Razer lived up to his words. When she came, he followed her within a few, smooth strokes. He let her thrashing body throw him over the edge into his climax, instead of pounding her into the mattress the way he wanted. When she quit trembling, Razer slid out, removing the condom and putting it in the trashcan by the bed. Beth shyly turned away, but Razer pulled her back onto his chest as he laid back.

While Beth lie panting on his chest, trying to catch her breath, her eyes fell to the only tattoo he had on his body. It was over his heart, which she thought was appropriate. The center had a Navy Seal insignia with a snake wrapping around it with other objects surrounding it. The items were two revolvers with a metal chain linking them, brass knuckles, a hand of cards and a razor knife. The whole tattoo had a smoky effect, which gave it a sinister appearance. It was when Beth saw the razor knife that she understood that the objects represented each of the eight, original members. Beth studied the razor knife closely and noticed it had several lines drawn into the pattern of the handle. On two lines there were two different dates.

"What is the significance of the dates on the razor?"

"The day I joined the Navy and the day I joined The Last Riders."

"What does your tattoo mean?"

"Everyone has to figure it out for themselves."

"Why do you only have this tattoo when everyone else has several more?"

Razer laughed. "I don't like needles. I was born addicted to crack and the first couple years I struggled just to stay alive. Doctors and nurses were always poking me with needles. I don't let them anywhere near me now, but I wanted this one. I'm not going to get another. I had to threaten the motherfucker who gave me this one not to tell anyone that I had passed out."

When Beth burst out laughing at that, Razer rolled her over, putting a hand over her mouth to cut the sound off.

"Shh... everyone will hear you laughing. They'll think you're laughing at my dick," he joked before removing his hand.

"I doubt that. Everyone here knows your dick is no laughing matter."

"Damn right," he gloated.

She wiggled out of his arms, grinning. "Of course, they might think I'm laughing at your fucking."

Razer lunged for her just as she rolled off the bed. Beth squealed like a girl and took off running to the bathroom with him chasing her.

"I doubt that. They heard you screaming when you came."

Razer pushed into the bathroom as she tried to slam the door. Jerking her into his arms, he kissed her silly. Beth's laughter died as he turned the shower on, maneuvering her into the warm spray. It seemed to be a night of first for her; sex and now showering with a man. As they washed each other, they explored one another's bodies until Razer broke away, leaving her under the water.

"Stay here."

He came back within minutes, joining her in the shower once more. At first she thought she was imagining what she saw glinting in his hand, but as she got a better look, she realized that she had been right.

"Razer... is that a straight razor?"

"Yes." Guiding her foot to the ledge in the shower where he helped her brace it there. He then grabbed some lotion hanging in the caddy beneath the showerhead. "Stand still."

He poured some lotion into the palm of his hand and rubbed it into the blond curls between her thighs before he raised the razor and gently began shaving.

"Razer, stop. I can…" She started to put her leg down.

"Don't move, I don't want to cut you," he warned.

Beth froze in place as he continued to shave her, moving her leg higher until he could even slide the Razer around the sides of her plump lips. It was definitely a new experience and Beth could only stand there blushing furiously. When he was done, he took the handheld showerhead down, aiming it between her legs until she was clean. Then he put it back and, taking another bottle down, poured a different lotion on his hand rubbing it gently into her cleanly shaven skin.

After he had finished, they got out of the shower and dried off before lazily making their way back into the bedroom. Beth then sat on the bed and called Lily while Razer went downstairs to bring some food back for them to eat.

As they ate, they sat talking about the likelihood of zombie apocalypses versus deep-sea volcano eruptions bringing an end to the world. When her giggling had her falling backwards, Razer took advantage of her splayed legs, pulling her towards him.

Beth knew by the look in his eyes that he wanted her again and she wanted him just as badly.

"I've had my dinner, now I want my dessert."

He kissed her thighs, sliding them apart in order to latch onto her clit. He took his time, determined to teach her the pleasure to be found in his bed. His tongue found her entrance and he laved inward, parting the lips of her pussy to taste the treasured tightness within. Beth's head fell back onto the pillow as her back arched, and she grabbed the rail at the head of his bed. Frantically, she tried to wrench away from him, the strength of her orgasm frightening. Razer held her firmly, his mouth latched onto her clit until her quivering stopped.

"I never knew I could come that hard," she whimpered.

Razer removed another condom from the nightstand and with a hand on her waist, flipped her boneless body onto her stomach.

"Now the challenge is for you to make me come as hard."

"So it's a challenge?"

"Not much of one, I'm almost ready to come." His hand forced her shoulders to the bed, which lifted her ass in the air. His sheathed cock slid inside her with a series of hard thrusts.

"You sore?"

"No"

"You will be. I took it easy on you last time." His hands on her hips had her pushing back against him hard. Loud slaps filled the air as he began pounding into her. Beth's hands reached out to grab the metal headboard to keep from banging her head against it. Beth's thighs began to tremble from the force he was fucking her with.

"Razer... I don't know if I can come again," Beth pleaded.

"You're going to come again harder than you did last time." Beth did not know if she would be able to take it if she did , however the force of his thrusts gradually rebuilt the fire inside of her body. He located the spot that sent her moaning and managed to continue to find it each time he surged inside her. Her pussy began tightening, gripping onto his length as Beth felt her climax building. She wasn't able to do much more than let Razer throw her into blazing contractions of sensation that had her grabbing a pillow to quiet the screams tearing from her throat.

Beth's orgasm had her rocking back onto him hard. Razer barely managed to pin her down so that he could finish with a series of thrusts that prolonged the pleasure building in his cock. Unable to draw it out any longer, he buried himself deep and came with a long groan.

"Woman, you take everything I have in me to keep up with you."

"Razer, I think you're the one trying to kill me."

CHAPTER TWELVE

Beth was surprised at how quickly the week went by while she stayed at Razer's house. Switching patients with Evie had made her days shorter, but of course, they were now longer for Evie. Beth felt guilty, yet could do little to change the situation until they discovered who had shot at her. Thankfully, next week they planned to switch again. Evie could go back to her original schedule, just different patients.

Friday was a light day for both of them, though Beth and Evie left the house early that morning. Evie was able to finish after one patient. Beth also finished early, returned to the house at lunchtime and headed into the kitchen for a bite to eat. As she entered the room, Rider was sitting at the counter, eating a sandwich.

Beth got the bread and began making herself a peanut butter sandwich. "The house is quiet. Where is everyone?"

Rider grinned. "It's Friday. Party day." At Beth's raised brow, he explained further, "Everyone went into town for supplies. Usually the guys go, but the girls went too this time. I heard them carrying on about something, but I try not to listen when they're scheming." He gave a shudder.

Beth laughed. She had become friends with several of

the house occupants. They respected her personal space and, when she hadn't responded to a few of their overtures, they had backed off with a smile. The thing that had surprised her the most was that, while they weren't shy about where or with whom they had sex, it wasn't as constant as she had thought.

They worked hard. Beth would hear them in the factory early in the mornings before she went to work and she'd noticed that they also worked late into the evenings. Often, they would come in exhausted only to grab a bite to eat before going to bed.

On the other hand, they were filled with sexual energy. Beth had walked in the living room or television room on several occasions to find the members having sex. Others who enjoyed watching would often join in if invited. Those were the ones that Beth had a harder time dealing with because she felt it was only a matter of time before she walked in to find Razer involved in another trio. The first couple of times she had immediately left the room, deeply embarrassed, however it didn't upset her as badly now. She supposed she was becoming desensitized.

Beth finished her sandwich and drank her milk then took her phone out to call Razer and see what he was doing. He had still been sleeping when she'd left; she hadn't wanted to wake him yet, but she now regretted missing the morning sex that she had become accustomed to. She was about to punch his phone number in when the front door opened and the men came in carrying groceries with the girls trailing behind, packing shopping bags from one of the few stores in town.

Evie raised her bag. "Beth you missed out; we emptied that excuse of a department store. After we get something to eat, we're going upstairs to change into our new clothes. Since I'm your best friend, I even picked you up a little something-something."

Beth laughed, lowering the phone as the kitchen became crowded with the guys putting up groceries and getting the meat ready for the grill.

"Watch it. Be careful." Beth's attention was drawn to Natasha whose hand was covering a patch on the curve of her breast. Beth froze, knowing in her gut what was underneath. Natasha went to the refrigerator and took out a soda. Opening it, she downed several swallows before sitting at the counter.

Her hand shaking, Beth put the phone back in her pocket. Face white, she headed for the door, wanting to get out of the room as quickly as possible.

Jewell drew everyone's attention to her. "What's wrong, Beth? You look like you're going to throw up."

"Where's Razer?" Beth's question came out in a whisper.

"He's not here, he's with…" Without waiting for Evie to finish, Beth tried to leave the room, but Evie grabbed her arm. "Let me get a cold rag."

"No, I have to get out of here."

"Leave her alone, Evie; she knows," Natasha said.

"Knows what?" Evie's confused eyes searched Beth's then went to Natasha.

"Fuck, no, he didn't. That's where you went while we were shopping?" Evie couldn't believe Razer's stupidity. The hurt on Beth's face was something she'd never wanted to see repeated and now it was right before her again.

"Yes." Natasha had guilt written all over her face.

"What date does it have?" Beth forced herself to look at Natasha expressionlessly.

"Today."

"Congratulations," Beth said, forcing herself to walk slowly out of the kitchen. She had her keys in the pocket of her pants and kept walking until she was out the front door.

Shade was getting off his bike when he saw Beth walk out the door. Even from where he was sitting, he could see the pain on her face. Quickly, he took out his cell, punching in Razer's number.

"Beth is leaving the house. From her face, I would say she knows what went down this morning."

"Keep her there. I'll be there in five." The line disconnected.

Beth did not run from the house. She consoled herself with the fact that at least this time she had not caught Razer in bed with another woman. No, it was tattooed on the woman's breast in plain sight so that every time Beth looked at her she would know the exact date that Razer had fucked her. As she drew closer to her car, she saw Shade leaning against the driver's door, blocking her from getting inside it.

"Hi, Beth."

"Shade."

Beth paused, waiting for him to move out of her way. When he didn't, she tried politely to get him to move.

"Excuse me, Shade, I would like to get in my car."

"Oh, going somewhere?"

As she was trying to get into her car, Beth figured that was pretty much self-evident, yet she still managed to respond, "Yes. Do you mind?" Again, she tried to get to the door of her car, but Shade would not budge.

"Actually, I do. Razer will be here in a minute. He wants you to wait for him."

"But I don't want to wait for Razer," Beth argued.

"Take that up with him." He shrugged.

"To do that, I would have to be here, which I don't want to be. Now, would you please move out of my way?"

"Too late." Shade gave a nod to Razer who had pulled in on his bike, deliberately blocking Beth's car. Shade moved away as Razer got off his bike to face an angry Beth.

"I want to leave and I would appreciate it if you would move your bike."

"Where are you going?"

"I need to see a patient."

"Who?"

Beth thought fast. "Mrs. Rogers."

Razer pulled out his cell phone. "What's her number? I want to see what the emergency is."

Beth couldn't think that fast. "Never mind. I don't have to tell you where I am going. I just am. Evie can bring my stuff when she comes to work Monday."

"So you're not planning on coming back?"

"No, I am not coming back," she snapped, irritated. "Why?"

"Why?" Beth repeated.

"Yes, Beth, why are you moving out, knowing that your life is in danger?" Razer responded.

"Because I don't want to stay here any longer."

"Why?"

"None of your fucking business," Beth said.

Razer's eyes narrowed at her words. "Watch yourself, Beth."

Beth glared back. "Fuck off!" She snatched her car door open, determined to run over his bike if he didn't move it, when she felt herself lifted off her feet and thrown over Razer's shoulder.

"I think we need to talk."

"I don't want to talk to you, you asshole. That was the whole point of me wanting to fucking leave!" Beth yelled.

"I wonder what Pastor Dean would think of the language spewing out of your mouth?"

"I don't fucking care! Let me go!" Beth screamed as he walked towards the house.

Razer ignored her and kept on walking. Beth saw various feet as they walked through the house, but none of them moved forward to help. She quit struggling as he walked up the stairs, figuring no argument was worth a broken neck , however as soon as he cleared the steps, her struggles resumed.

"What is your problem?" Beth yelled at him the second her feet touched the floor in Razer's room.

He raised a sardonic brow at her as he shut the door,

leaning back against it to prevent her leaving before they'd had a chance to talk.

"I think you're the one who obviously has a problem since you're determined to leave without giving me an explanation."

"I certainly don't owe you any explanations."

"You have been lying in that bed, fucking my brains into mush for a week, woman. I damn well think I *do* deserve an explanation."

"I know you fucked Natasha," Beth said, simply wanting to get it over with so she could leave before bursting into tears in front of the jerk.

"Did she say I fucked her?"

"No, but she didn't deny it."

Razer nodded. 'That's because Viper asked her not to."

"Viper?"

"Yes. He was here this morning before everyone got up. I had a meeting with him. No one other than Shade, Natasha, me and now you, know that Viper is in town. He wants to keep it that way for a little while longer."

"So Viper and Natasha?"

"Viper fucked Natasha this morning and afterwards she got her tat."

Beth felt relief. As if she could finally breathe again.

"That doesn't mean I didn't enjoy the show." Beth's breath caught again. Feeling as if her legs were going to give out, she walked the short distance to sit on the end of the bed.

"You watched?"

"Yes, but I did not touch or participate," Razer clarified. "Beth, I told you no woman has her name on my dick. That means you, too. What we have is good and I am not ready for it to end and I don't think you are, either." He waited for a nod from her before he continued, "That being said, I know me touching another woman in the club goes beyond what you can deal with, so I am giving you my word that I won't touch, but I am not going to let you cut my balls off, either. So you will have to deal with me watching and enjoying the others playing." Beth didn't know how to feel about his blunt reply.

Razer watched her facial expressions and sought to relieve her fears. "I am not going to do shit behind your back. If I watch Rider give it to Jewell, I'm not going to pretend I didn't. But I know you enjoy watching, too, Beth. You didn't exactly run out of the room the other day when Knox and Natasha were fucking and you sure as hell didn't turn your eyes away last night when Bliss gave Rider a blowjob. You may leave the room, but not without taking your sweet time. Instead, when we went to bed last night, you were so primed that it took me half the night to satisfy you and that's saying a lot coming from me, which is also why I was still sleeping when you left."

Beth turned bright red. He was right, watching Bliss and Rider the night before had brought out the desires in her body and she had thought it would never be quenched. Razer had produced several satisfying climaxes in her and had doused the fire that had been brought to life by observing them. As soon as Beth admitted that to herself, recriminations set in. She could hear her father screaming in her head how sick and perverted she was.

As if he could tell what was going on in her head, Razer softly said, "No, Beth." He then got on his knees before her and pulled her hands away from her face. "There is nothing wrong with enjoying sex in all the different ways there are to enjoy it. There is no one underage here, coerced or forced to be here. We enjoy sex and have a lifestyle that works for us. However, I can see that goes against everything you have been raised to believe and want for yourself. You have to find out what suits you best and makes you happy."

Beth took a deep breath. "I can deal with you watching. I just don't want to be worried that you're going to fuck another woman the minute I leave your side."

Razer didn't say he would not touch another woman

ever, however he was able to give her some peace of mind. "I promise that before I touch another woman, I will tell you. I don't want that fear in you all the time, but I will tell you, knowing that when I do, we will be over because I'm also aware that you couldn't deal with that choice from me. Okay?"

It was as good as she was going to get. Beth knew she would have to be content with what he was able to give her. "All right."

"Are we cool?"

Beth smiled. "Yes."

Razer leaned forward, giving her a deep kiss. As Beth responded by winding her arms around his neck, a knock at the door interrupted them.

Razer disengaged their lips, standing up. Before answering the door, he warned her, "Remember, no one is supposed to know that it wasn't me who voted Natasha in this morning." At her nod, Razer opened the door to see Evie standing uncertainly, ready to knock again.

"Can I come in?"

Razer opened the door wider in invitation. Evie searched both of their faces before a smile lit her face, determining that for now their argument had been settled. She then lifted her hand with a bag in it. "I got you an outfit when we went out today. I knew you didn't have anything here to wear for the party tonight. I would've swung by your house and picked you up something, but figured you didn't have anything there, either." She laughed. "So I took care of it when I picked up something new for myself."

"You shouldn't have, but thanks. I appreciate that you picked something out for me."

Evie smirked, handing her the bag. "Yes, well, you'll probably wish that I hadn't when you see what I bought. I'm getting out of here before you do. I have to get ready myself. If you don't hurry, the guys will pick out all the best steaks for themselves."

"I'll get changed and be right down." Impulsively, Beth grabbed a startled Evie, giving her a tight hug.

"Girl, you know I don't hug," she said, pulling herself away with a smile.

"I just wanted you to know how much your friendship means to me," Beth said, not in the least fazed.

"God, now she is getting mushy. I definitely gotta go." Beth laughed as Evie practically ran from the room.

Razer shut the door behind her, taking Beth into his arms. His lips brushed her neck.

"How come you never get mushy with me?" he questioned.

"Because unlike Evie, who ran from the room, you would pass out in horror." Beth giggled.

"Try me," Razer said seductively. "I might surprise you."

Beth blushed, stepping back out of his arms to pick up the bag with the clothes Evie had given her and grabbing a towel.

"I doubt it. A man who commands complete dominion over where his dick goes is not ready for mushy." At his laughter, Beth stuck her tongue out at him before slamming the bathroom door, hiding from his questioning gaze.

The shower relaxed her nerves , so Beth used the time to psych herself up for the night ahead. Evie had warned her that gatherings on Friday's were used to provide a variety of entertainment. Beth remembered the first night she had visited with Razer and was well aware of what she was in for tonight. The surprising part was that she felt no fear; nervous excitement, though? Yes. Beth had become familiar with the members now and with it the rules of the club. Participation was always voluntary, if a person didn't want to join in, then no attempt was made to force them. If one of the women did not want to have sex with a particular member, then that was also fine. That was probably why the club worked so well, everyone's wishes were respected.

Beth dried off and opened the bag of clothes Evie had purchased for her.

"No way." Beth started to put the clothes back in the bag, but Evie's face as she handed them to her had her hesitating. She bit her lip, not knowing what to do. Beth didn't want to hurt Evie's feelings, yet she certainly couldn't wear the clothes.

"Dammit." With an aggravated sigh, Beth put the clothes on and then nervously turned to look at herself in the bathroom mirror. The blue jean skirt barely covered her ass. It did, however, cover it, Beth assured herself. The skirt had black leather patches that matched the top, which is what had Beth really blushing. It was a black leather vest that covered her breasts, but it left her breastbone completely bare. It had no buttons, only a metal clasp that formed a circle right above her belly button. Critically, Beth stared at herself. It was certainly form fitting and the leather clung lovingly to the full curves of her breasts, though they weren't exposed. What was exposed was her midriff and tummy by the skirt riding low on her hips.

It exposed less than a swimsuit and it would look more conservative than what Beth remembered some of the girls wearing. A sharp knock on the door startled her out of her argument with herself about grabbing a t-shirt and jeans.

"Let's go. I'm hungry."

Beth opened the door and Razer's reaction settled the argument. At least she knew he appreciated the way she looked. Lust was plain as day on his face.

"I'm ready," Beth said nervously, smoothing the skirt down.

"Yes, you are." Razer nodded his head and started to reach for her.

"Oh, no. You said you were hungry and so am I. My lunch was interrupted and now I'm starved."

"Baby, I can satisfy that hunger right after I satisfy—"

Beth shook her head, laughing at him.

"All right then, but you are going to make it up to me later," Razer warned.

"Don't I always?" Beth joked. She grew serious as a quick look passed over Razer's face, however it was gone before she could decipher it. Thinking she imagined it, Beth snuggled against him as he placed an arm around her shoulders, leading her out of the bedroom.

As Beth moved forward towards the stairs, Razer held her still while he turned and locked the bedroom door with a key he pulled from his pocket. He had never locked his bedroom door before.

"Friday night the beds run short; I want to make sure mine is empty when I want it." Nervousness filled her at his reminder of the activities that the members would become involved in as the night progressed. Before she could run back in her room and change clothes, Razer turned her towards the stairs.

Coning into the living room, the party was in full swing. Beth looked around, realizing that several people were there that she did not recognize.

"I'm going to go check on the steaks," Razer said, releasing her as they both spotted Evie and Jewell making a huge salad.

"I'll help Evie and Jewell," Beth said as Razer snagged a beer from the cooler sitting on the table before going outside.

Evie gave Beth a bright smile as she approached the counter.

"You look great!"

Beth smiled at her eager expression, happy that she had made the decision to wear the clothes.

"You look fabulous," she complimented in return.

Evie was wearing black leather bootie shorts and a leather corset that laced up the top; but it was the thigh high leather boots that placed her in the hot category. She looked sexy and confident with her dark brown hair loose and flowing around her sultry face. Evie stood out among the women swarming the room.

Evie noticed Beth's glances and explained. "On Friday nights, the club allows members to bring in hang-arounds."

"Hang-arounds?"

"Women or men that want to hang around the club to party or fuck. If we like them and they are interested, they can become a probate. "

"If they don't?"

"Then they're like Sam, they stay for the sex or leave because it's not for them. We don't take many probates, only one or two a year."

"Are they always female?" Beth stared at one particular woman who was already sitting on Rider's lap, grinding herself against him.

Evie laughed. "I brought Knox in, but he was military, stationed where I was at. All the other guys are ex-military and knew each other in the service. That's why they trust each other so much."

Beth nodded, remembering Razer's tattoo. Reaching for the celery and picking up a knife, she began cutting it and placing it in the salad bowl that they were working on to feed the huge crowd.

"Don't the female members get jealous with the new women here on Fridays?" Beth still couldn't understand how they managed to keep their feelings separate.

Evie and Jewell shared a glance. "No. If we did, we wouldn't last long and we sure as hell wouldn't have become members. We're a motorcycle club that enjoys sexual freedom. We don't do that by putting restraints on each other."

Jewell sighed and laid down the lettuce she was shredding. "What she's trying to tell you without freaking you out is that we enjoy the new bitches, too. It's hot as hell to watch them get fucked senseless; we even join in if we want. Hell, girl, these guys can go all night. There's plenty for everyone."

"Shut up, Jewell."

Before Beth could be further embarrassed, Razer and the guys walked in with a massive tray of steaks and hamburgers. Pandemonium ensued with everyone going for the food at the same time. She dodged several elbows as she got out of the way of the starving horde until the line thinned out. She grinned as Razer handed her a plate with a steak already on it.

"Gotta take care of my girl; she's going to need her strength for later."

Beth took her plate, averting her eyes from him. She didn't want him to see the pleasure his words had brought welling to the surface. She knew he hadn't meant it the way it sounded, but Beth couldn't help her reaction. When she looked up, she saw Evie giving her a concerned look. Beth quickly moved away, placing a small amount of salad on her plate.

Razer snagged them a couple of chairs at the table and they ate leisurely. Evie had followed them over and brought her a beer. They sat chatting in their small group until the volume of the music from the front room had risen and the loud voices drew her attention. The darkness outside showed they had lost track of time as they sat there talking.

"I think the party has started," Evie said with a mischievous grin.

Razer took their plates to the kitchen while Beth threw away their empty bottles. Everyone tried to clean up after themselves, not leaving the responsibility to any one person. Beth didn't think other clubs did this, yet she admired it, thinking it showed the respect they held for each other. *Or,* she thought, laughing to herself, *the women would kick their asses before they were treated like servants.*

Razer's arm went around her shoulders as he steered her into the large living room. This time, she wasn't stunned by the scene that met her eyes. The furniture had been pulled back into a couple of grouping areas or lined up against the wall, leaving the middle of the floor bare. The empty area was now filled with dancing couples gyrating against each other.

Evie was snagged around her waist by Crash as they walked through the doorway. The last Beth saw, her legs were wrapped around his waist and they were trying to see who could find each other's tonsils first.

Out of the corner of her eye, Beth saw Jewell being dragged down onto Knox's lap, who already had the redhead's top off. Jewell giggled, quickly evening the playing field by pulling off her t-shirt.

Razer's arm tightened around her as he felt her stiffening next to him. Maneuvering them to the dance floor, his hand cupped her ass as he started moving her to the beat of the music. The close proximity of his body stirred Beth's desire. The beat of the music allowed her to loosen the tight control she held herself in. She gradually relaxed her body and swayed provocatively against his and, when his lips found hers, her pussy grew wet just thinking about going to their room later that night.

"Want to get a drink?" Razer asked after the third song.

Beth nodded gratefully. The huge bar set up on one side of the room was empty and Beth moved behind it to get their drinks. Wanting water to quench her thirst, she made herself an ice-cold glass and reached into the cooler to find a cold beer for Razer. She watched as he leaned against the bar next to her, drinking the frigid liquid. They simply stood there for a moment as it was the least crowded spot in the whole room.

Every now and then someone would come up and ask for a drink. Beth grinned at Razer while she played bartender. Razer would even hand out a few since several wanted them at the same time. Having fun, Beth took a drink of her water and almost spit it out when she saw the man standing against the wall with Bliss, Echo and Dawn, all vying for his attention. The large man with sandy blond hair was ignoring the women. His arms, which were folded across his chest, exhibited bulging biceps that were clearly visible beneath his tight, black t-shirt. The black motorcycle pants and boots highlighted the sexiness he exuded without his ever having to make a move. Yet what had Beth choking on her drink was that she recognized him.

Cash Adams had been a member of her church when she had been a young girl. She remembered staring at him, thinking how handsome he was and that he must be what her father preached about when he talked about sins of the flesh. Even as a young girl, he had awakened her body to stirrings she had been too ashamed to acknowledge. She hadn't been alone; every woman that he crossed paths with had a hungry look come into their eyes. He was born into a family that didn't have much, but Cash never lacked for money and everyone knew it was from his grandmother's bootlegging. His parents, as God-fearing members of the church, had refused her help, however they hadn't been able to keep Cash from accepting what money his grandmother gave him.

As he got older, he even began working for her. He became an expert at evasion not only from the police, but also from the male members in the community who were angered at his lack of restraint when it came to nailing anything he was offered. The women threw themselves at him with an amazing lack of decorum for the chance to be in his bed. After one public fight he had disappeared. Cash had beaten an irate brother who had been angry over his sister's deflowerment, which the whole town knew about because the stupid girl had bragged to her best friend, who also had a big mouth. What made it worse was that she had also been with Cash.

Everyone had assumed he had finally pissed the wrong person off and had been killed. In truth, he had hidden in the vast mountain region. He was good at that and Beth had never believed he was dead, she had known better.

"That's Cash Adams." Beth couldn't keep the awe out

of her voice.

Razer came up behind her as she stood behind the bar. "I take it you know him?"

"He went to my church before he disappeared."

"From what he told us, he left town to join the Navy, which is where he met Viper and the rest of us. He's Viper's lieutenant. He rode in with him this morning."

"He hasn't changed, I see."

"No?"

Beth could only nod her head speechlessly as Cash smiled at her. He said something before leaving the women standing, waiting like little puppies for their master's return.

"Razer," he said and Razer nodded. Cash's eyes then found Beth. "You're Beth Cornett, Pastor Cornett's daughter?"

"Yes." Beth couldn't hide her surprise that he recognized her.

"You're all grown up, I see." His blue eyes brushed the cleavage that was accented by the leather vest.

"You have, too." She stated the obvious. His facial features had toughened and matured into a face that was compelling to look at.

He smiled. "I heard about your dad and mom. Sorry to hear of your loss."

"Thanks."

"I'm just sorry the bastard is dead because I wish he was still alive so I could beat the shit out of him."

Beth's mouth dropped open at his bluntness.

Razer reached back and handed Cash a beer, which Cash took, twisted the top off and took a drink from before continuing, "He was a sick fuck that I was too young to know how to put out of commission. That wouldn't be the case today."

"No, I don't imagine it is," Beth agreed, not knowing what else to say.

"Good seeing you again." He gave Razer a nod and

stepped away, again enveloped in the midst of the three women.

"Wow."

"Careful, I could get jealous," Razer said with a grin.

Beth looked over her shoulder to see he was only joking before turning again to watch Cash as he went back to standing against the wall. His brown eyes surveyed the room almost as if he was searching for someone. He gave the women occasional replies to keep them pacified, but he never diverted his concentration from the room.

Razer leaned in against her, fitting himself to her back so that his cock was pressed against her ass as his arm slid around her waist. The pressure of his body forced her against the bar and held her in place. Beth's eyes looked around the room, trying to find what Cash was searching for, but her task was forgotten as her attention was caught by the activities going on in the room. Members were stroking and sucking various body parts and openly fucking. Beth had been so surprised by the appearance of Cash, she had failed to notice the sexual activities going on in the room before now.

Stori was sitting on Memphis's lap, fucking herself on his cock. He was holding her by the waist and was jerking her up and down his shaft as she faced him with her legs pushed back and the heels of her feet on the chair behind his head. Memphis moved her up and down faster on his slick cock while Beth watched as Stori's head fell back, giving total control over to Memphis.

"I'm glad you enjoy watching, too." Razer's thumb reached up to stroke her nipple through the leather, raising the nub to a hard, aching peak.

Beth didn't say anything, she simply stood there as his thumb began its torment.

"As you can deduce, Stori is very limber. That's how she got her nickname. Because every member had a story to tell about the position she could get you off in."

"Her nickname?" Beth said in confusion.

"Yeah, the guys name the women." His rough jaw nudged her head towards Evie who was on her knees in the corner sucking off Train. His hands were making a mess of the woman's hair as he used it to guide her on his cock. "Evie was given her name because she is so... so... tempting." Razer's hand that had been holding the ice-cold beer slid under her skirt to pull her panties aside, finding her already slickened clit. His ice cold touch had her standing on tippy toes, trying to get away at first, then seconds later to guide him in his movements.

Beth felt self-conscious momentarily until she realized that no one could see Razer's movements behind the enclosed bar. His hand that had been tormenting her nipple left to raise the back of her skirt, showing the thong she wore. The tiny pink strip was barely visible between her creamy butt cheeks.

His hand returned to her midriff, his thumb again finding her nipple as his hips pressed into her without the smooth leather between her ass and his jean-covered cock. She unconsciously wiggled back against him as he rubbed and stroked her clit while hidden from view by the rest of the room by the tall bar. Unable to help herself, her head fell back onto his shoulder.

"Ember?" Again his cheek nudged her, this time towards the strawberry blond that was sitting by Nickel, drinking a beer and casually talking as if nothing was going on around her. "She's slow to start, but when she does, her pussy is like an inferno."

Beth was close to climaxing due to Razer seducing her with his words and fingers. No one looking at them would know what was going on behind the bar. The illusion of privacy allowed Beth to participate without the guilt of recriminations storming her, drowning out everything she believed herself incapable of doing.

Her head moved of its own accord to Jewell who was sitting on Knox's lap with the other woman. She was kissing the other woman while casually stroking Knox's cock through his pants. The three were in their own little world. As she watched, one by one they stood and walked to the stairway.

"Jewell was given her name because her…" his hand in her panties pressed roughly against her clit before two fingers pressed against it tightly. Holding it in a firm clasp that didn't hurt; it simply prevented her from climaxing, which is what she was about to finally accomplish. "…is like a precious ruby, all red and glistening when you're going down on her."

A whimper escaped and her hand shakily reached out to grasp the bar. When she finally managed to gain momentary control, her eyes once again fell to Cash and the three women. They were getting tired of being ignored. Not long after her gaze had stared back to them, Echo flounced off and was soon on the lap of another member, while Dawn, with a pout, found a seat next to Sam, who, for once, was sitting by herself with a bottle of whiskey in her hands.

Bliss, also disheartened, turned to leave, but with a snap of his wrist, Cash pulled her back. The small woman was lifted off her feet and, within the blink of an eye, was pressed back against the wall he had been leaning on with her legs wrapped around his lean waist. Two of Razer's fingers suddenly drove deep within her and he begin thrusting harder. She rose even higher on her toes as she watched Cash's hands adjust his pants to pull out his hardened cock, placing a condom on just before he shoved it into a withering Bliss, who was obviously having issues accepting his large cock. The woman arched as he fucked her hard. Beth thought he might be too rough, considering the pounding she was taking, but the look on her face was one of ecstasy, not pain.

"Now, Bliss, I can't give an informed opinion about, but the men say that her pussy is like dying and going to Heaven."

With a scissoring motion of his fingers and a brush of

his thumb against her clit, she came. She raised her hand and bit into it to keep from screaming and drawing everyone's eyes to her. When Beth's spasms stopped, Razer removed his fingers gently, smoothing down her skirt before stepping away to wash his hands in the sink behind them.

Beth picked up her glass, taking a long drink and trying to calm her body down when a half-empty whiskey bottle appeared on the counter in front of her.

"Come on, Razer, I'm bored. Let's go upstairs and play. You can come back down here later." She waved her hand at Beth "She can come, too. I'll show her how you really like it."

"Get gone, Sam," Razer said, turning back from the sink.

Sam narrowed her eyes. "Since when do you say no to a threesome? Damn, girl, maybe we need to go upstairs so you can show me a thing or two. All this time I thought you were a tight-ass, little virgin. You been getting it and keeping it a secret?"

Sam reached out for the whiskey bottle, however Razer took it away, setting it back behind the counter where she couldn't reach it.

"You know the rules. You can't get drunk or you're escorted home. You ready to leave?"

"I am not drunk." With a shrug, she gave Beth a sweet smile that didn't reach her hardened eyes. "I can find someone else to play with tonight. Maybe tomorrow, Razer? I need a little maintenance work from you."

"What does she mean?" Razer gave Sam an angry glare, but didn't try to stop her explaining.

"Don't tell me Razer hasn't showed off his special skill with that razor of his. He keeps all the girls nice and neat. Buys special lotions for just that purpose; he's an expert at it, he never nicks the flesh. He always does it before he goes down on you." Sam could see she had struck her target a huge blow. "Later, Razer."

The women both knew Razer would be back in her bed, it was only a matter of time. Beth tried hard not to throw up, bringing a shaking hand up to cover her face until she could regain control.

"Ignore the bitch," Razer said calmly.

"Please, don't touch me," Beth begged. She removed her hand to see Cash looking at her in concern. Bliss, now covered, was also watching her with a sympathetic look.

Bending down, Razer lifted Beth up and her legs automatically went around his waist while her arms circled his neck. He carried her upstairs to his room, bracing her against the wall as he unlocked the door. Finally getting her hurt emotions under control, she glanced down the hall and saw several doors open.

"Why are the doors open?"

"Curious kitten?"

"I was just wondering, usually they're closed."

"It means that anyone who wants to watch or participate is welcome."

"Oh." Beth buried her face in his neck.

Razer laughed at her shyness as he carried her through the doorway. "Want me to leave the door open?" he teased.

Beth shook her head in his neck and the door closed with a sharp snap before she was lowered gently to the bed. "You always going to be this shy?"

Beth studied his face "Does it bother you?"

"No, it doesn't bother me," he reassured her, raising her to a sitting position. Razer's hands went to the clasp of her top to unsnap it, yet her hand grabbed his to stop him.

"Beth, what Sam said wasn't all true. I am not a day spa."

"Not all true, but most of it. I think I'm angry with myself, not you. It was obvious you were experienced at shaving a woman, but I buried my head in the sand. I do that a lot with you." She raised her hand when he would have interrupted her. "Please, let me finish. I don't expect anything from you except for you to keep your promise and break it off with me before touching another woman again. I can accept it while it lasts if I know I am the only one, even if it's only for a short time."

"I can do that." Razer reached out, brushing a thumb across her pale cheek. "Now it's my turn. I haven't touched Sam or Evie since that night. I am not saying I haven't been with other women, just not those two. I couldn't when I realized how bad I'd hurt you. I wouldn't do that to you again."

Reaching up, she cupped his face in her hands. "Razer, I know I'm not as good as the other women you have been with, I can try harder if you show me what—"

His mouth silenced her, reassuring her without words, but Beth scooted away from him to sit in the middle of the bed on her knees.

"Come here."

Beth shook her head no, moving out of his grasp when Razer would have reached for her. Stopping when she reached the head of the bed, she stood up, removing her top and throwing it on the chair beside the bed. She reached for her skirt, wiggling out of it provocatively and letting it join the top.

"Does Kitty wanna play?" Razer pulled his shirt, his boots and then his jeans off. When he reached for her, she dodged him again, dancing across the bed.

"Woman, are you thinking about teasing me after I watched practically the whole club getting off and you came on my fingers? I don't think so." With a lunge, he reached out, snagging her ankles when she thought he would go for her arms.

As her feet were pulled neatly out from under her, Beth felt herself falling softly on the bed. With a jerk, he pulled her towards him until her ass was on the edge of the bed. Her fingers grasped the edge, afraid she would fall off.

With one hand he brought both of her legs to lay against his shoulders. The panties she wore were snapped apart as he tugged sharply.

"I am going to make you purr and then I am going to make you scream." Beth was getting worried she had bitten off more than she could chew from the look on Razer's face.

His fingers found her wet and slick. Taking his cock in his hand, he guided it to her entrance and plunged deep into her pussy with one, hard stroke.

A gasp escaped her at the pleasure she felt when he began to thrust within her. Always before he had controlled himself and, while not rough tonight, he also didn't treat her as if she would break. Beth realized he had been holding back, afraid of frightening her. Razer had been taking it easy on her, not truly giving himself because she had been a virgin when they had first had sex. She was certain he had not been enjoying the sex they had been sharing as much as her if he was having to restrain himself. Beth remembered the look on his face from earlier tonight when she had joked him about always keeping him satisfied.

Driven from the pleasure with her thoughts, Razer realized she wasn't with him. With her legs still over his one shoulder, he leaned over her, tightening her pussy on his cock. They both groaned at the added stimulation and his thrusts became shorter as if she was clutching him, not wanting to let go.

"Razer?"

"Kitty is going to see how Razer likes to play tonight."

Leaning back, he took her legs in his hands and brought them straight up, opening and closing them in a scissoring motion at the same time that he pumped his hips, making his cock delve deeper into her sheath than he had ever achieved before.

Her climax was earth shattering when it hit. Rubbing her clit, he prolonged her release until she lay trembling. While she was unable to stop the spasms going through her, Razer's thrusts escalated. Her legs were now wrapped around his waist as his hands guided the movements of her hips.

With a groan, she felt him jerk within her, coming hard. When he was done, he pulled out and moved her until she lay in the middle of the bed. She could only lie there, trying to catch her breath with Razer having just as much trouble getting his breath back to normal. Finally, he was able to remove the condom, placing it in the trashcan.

He went into the bathroom and Beth heard the water running before it was shut off. He returned with a wet washcloth to unabashedly wash her before taking the washcloth back to the bathroom. When Razer lay down beside her on the bed, his hand massaged her still trembling muscles.

"Still sensitive?"

"Yes." Blushing, she looked away, but Razer turned her face back to his with a firm finger.

"There's nothing to be embarrassed about. Did you enjoy yourself?"

"You know I did."

"So did I. When you fuck, it's going to get messy. If not, then something's not working right. The aftermath of sex can be just as sexy as the getting to it part. I like them both. I want you to get on the pill, okay? If we're going to be exclusive, I want to come in you."

"I'll make an appointment Monday."

"I get tested regularly even though I always wear a condom, but I'll get a new one before I go naked. Deal?"

"Deal."

Razer turned out the light, lying on his side, pulling her close and cupping her breast in his hand with his head buried in her throat.

She felt him relaxing as a thought occurred to her. "Razer?"

"Yes?" his voice already sounded sleepy.

"Can we go for a ride on your bike tomorrow?"

"Yes, kitten, now go to sleep."

She snuggled against him, already planning on where they would go the following day.

CHAPTER THIRTEEN

She woke Razer up at eight, unable to control her excitement. Beth ignored his grumpy mood, which disappeared when she bravely jumped in the shower with him, determined to become the woman that would be able to keep Razer satisfied. The look on his face was worth the embarrassment and the orgasm he gave her in return made her body practically sing.

Beth made them eggs and toast. She was pouring coffee when Shade walked through the back door and took a seat on a stool by Razer.

"Hey Shade, where were you last night?" Beth asked.

Shade paused, about to take a sip from the coffee cup he had swiped from Razer with a glare. Beth laughed. Getting another cup, she poured another one for Razer.

"Yeah, Shade, where were you last night?" Razer aggravated his hung-over friend.

"I was visiting a sick friend," he said with a straight face.

"That was kind of you. Do they need any help? I could go down before we go for a ride," concerned, Beth offered, seeing Shade was obviously tired.

"No, thanks," Shade's reply was strangled.

"Are you all right? You sound as if you're coming down with something. Is your friend contagious?"

"No. If I need any help, I'll ask Evie. They know each other very well."

"You do that. Evie will stay on top of the situation."

"Yes, she will," Razer heartily agreed.

Shade's shoulders slumped. "Why are you both up so early?"

Beth smiled brightly at Shade. "Razer is taking me for a ride this morning."

Beth set a plate in front of Shade who looked down at it, a little baffled. "I thought you might be hungry," Beth said, taking a bite from her smaller breakfast. It was obvious she had given him most of her own portion.

Shade started to slide the plate back towards her, but the disappointed look on her face had him picking up the fork and taking a bite gingerly. After being up all night, partying, he had been heading to bed when he had walked in from the backyard and saw them in the kitchen. Seeing Razer in his riding clothes, he had been curious as to where they were going, but now he was wishing his boots had kept on walking.

"Where to?"

"If it's okay with Razer, I thought we could ride to see my sister?"

"Cool with me," Razer said, finishing his breakfast and taking mercy on his friend. He slid Shade's plate towards him and began eating his food.

"Mind if I ride along?" Shade asked, trying to keep the small bite of egg he had forced down to stay in his heaving stomach.

"I don't mind, but…" Beth frowned, trailing off.

"What?"

"Don't be surprised if my sister is a little nervous around you," Beth said, not wanting to hurt Shade's feelings.

"Any reason why?" Shade probed.

147

A curtain fell over Beth's face. "Probably the whole biker aura."

Razer finished eating and poured himself another coffee. "Finish eating, Beth, so we can get on the road. Lily will be fine. She needs to get used to the biker aura. The sooner the better."

Beth started to argue with him, to tell him her sister didn't adjust well, however she ended up merely shrugging to herself. It was really none of his business and it would only force her to make more explanations, which she really did not want to do.

It was a beautiful day. The motorcycles flew down the road and, from what Razer yelled at Shade, they were going WFO; whatever that meant. Beth appreciated the expert way Razer handled his bike on the winding roads. It was obvious Shade and he had ridden many times together, each knowing what the other would do beforehand.

When they were halfway to Lily's college, they stopped for gas. Beth was standing, watching the men pump gas when the roar of bikes filled the air. Five motorcycles road into the gas station and the men in the group gave Razer and Shade hard stares. As they passed to park at the side of the store, four women that had been riding on the back of the bikes climbed off as the men stood, lighting cigarettes.

"I need to go to the restroom." Razer gave her a curt nod of acknowledgement, hanging up the nozzle.

When she came out of the restroom, Beth found herself surrounded by the women with the bikers.

"Hi." Beth smiled amicably.

The women stared back in confusion, their threatening glares disappearing.

"You guys out for a ride? It's a beautiful day, isn't it? I love your jacket; where did you get it?" The awe in her voice wasn't feigned as she stared at the black and red leather jacket the woman was wearing. "I have a pink one, but it's not as nice as yours."

"Thanks," the one with the leather jacket was finally able to get in a word.

"My name is Beth."

"Is she for real?" one female biker asked.

Beth looked at the one who spoke. "Where did you get your hair done? I have been wanting my hair like that for forever." She touched her own fine, silky hair, staring enviously at the red-haired woman's glorious curls.

At that, the ice was broken and the women introduced themselves as "Crazy Bitch", "Sex Piston", "KillyaMa", and "Fat Louise". Beth could only gape as each woman introduced herself.

"You haven't been warming back long, have you, bitch?" the one called Sex Piston asked.

"Warming back?"

"Are you for real?" KillyaMa repeated sex Piston's earlier question. She reached out and poked her in the arm, forcing Beth to take a step back.

"Cool it. We don't want to start no trouble," Fat Louise said.

"It's fine, no offense taken. I know she was just joking." Beth smiled reassuringly. Feeling another poke at her back, Beth turned to see Sex Piston.

"She's for fucking real."

"Well, it's been nice meeting you. I better get back. We're on the way to see my sister. She goes to Breckenridge College."

"That explains it."

"Explains what?"

"Nothing. Better get going. Your man will be waiting."

Impulsively, Beth pulled out the pen and paper that she always carried in her purse.

"Text me sometime. I hope we can get to know each other better. What is your club's name?"

"Destructors." No one reached out to take the paper with Beth's phone number.

"Oh, that's cool."

"Your man's?"

"The Last Riders." Even Beth wasn't oblivious to the respectful look that appeared on their faces.

Sex Piston snatched the paper from Beth's hand. "We'll keep in touch."

Beth smiled and hurried back to the bikes. "Sorry I took so long."

Getting on behind Razer, she noticed Shade had cut his lip, but the drone of the other bikers leaving distracted her from asking if there had been trouble. Beth reminded herself to ask Razer later. Another hour ride and they pulled up in front of Lily's dorm. The men patiently waited outside as Beth went inside to surprise Lily. It took several knocks before Lily opened her door; she only answered it after Beth called her name.

"Beth." Lily threw herself into her sister's arms.

"Lily, what's going on?" Concerned, Beth drew her sister inside and sat her down in the only chair in the small room.

"Nothing." Proving her words to be a lie, she burst into tears.

"Don't tell me nothing is wrong. I want the truth, Lily," Beth said firmly.

"I just don't fit in here, Beth. All the girls hate me and the boys just stare. It creeps me out. I wanted to come home, but you said I couldn't."

Beth felt terrible. She had been trying to protect Lily from whoever was trying to kill her, so she had wanted Lily to stay at college until it was safe, but she could see that had been the wrong move. She should have come down and spent the weekend with her. Lily had to have stability in her life because, if anything changed, it frightened her. Once again she was reminded that her father's rules that had stymied Beth's emotional growth, were the same rules that had been a lifesaver for Lily, giving her the feeling of being protected and loved.

Beth had carefully been working on loosening the

control Lily needed while at the same time trying to encourage her to spread her wings. Instead, it had made Lily feel lost and alone in a new environment. She wasn't flourishing, she was retreating.

"Well, I am here today. We're going to go out to lunch and do a little shopping."

Lily's bright smile rewarded her efforts. "Let me get my purse." Lily threw herself in Beth arms, this time with a beautiful smile. "I am so happy you came to see me. I have missed you so much." As Lily let Beth go, she grabbed her purse from the desk.

Beth took her sister's hand. "I didn't exactly come alone. A couple of friends brought me."

"Evie?" Lily liked Evie; they had developed a guarded friendship.

"No, Razer and Shade. You remember the men who gave us a ride home when you were released from the hospital?"

"Why would they bring you?"

"Well, I am kind of seeing Razer. I really like him, Lily, and I want you to like him also. I swear they won't do anything to make you uncomfortable or I wouldn't have let them come." Lily trusted her sister, even though the thought of being near the two men made her sick. Beth never asked anything of her in return for taking care of her. If Beth wanted her to get to know her friends, then it was important that she try.

"Then I am sure I will like him, too." Lily squeezed her sister's hand in return.

"Good."

When the women walked outside hand in hand, Razer and Shade could only stare. They were still just as awestruck by their beauty as they had been the first time they'd seen them together. One was so light and golden, her smile as bright as the sun. Her loving nature was obvious as she held her sister's nervous hand. The other, a dark enigma that only let her guard down when she looked at her sister. The male students walking by stopped, appreciating the beauty walking among them. The female students, on the other hand, were not as appreciative.

"Bet you a six pack those bitches hate her guts," Shade muttered.

Shade let his gaze catch several of the men and women and they all soon hurried on their way, smart enough to know they were out of their league.

Beth smiled at Razer and Shade.

"Lily, you remember Razer and Shade."

"Hello."

"I told Lily we could go eat lunch. Maybe a little shopping if it won't put you guys out."

"Not at all. You girls climb on the bikes."

Beth climbed on the back of Razer's bike, but started to get back off, noticing Lily had not moved. Razer's hand on her thigh stopped her.

"Stay put."

"Come here, Lily," Shade ordered.

Lily's body tautened and she threw a wild look at her sister. Before Beth could do anything, Shade threw his extra helmet at her.

"Get on the bike. I'm hungry. Move that sweet ass or I'll put you on the bike myself." Lily got on the bike, putting on the helmet as Shade started it up and they pulled out with a roar of motors.

The restaurant they chose was small with a family atmosphere. They sat talking after they'd eaten until the waitress started throwing them dirty looks. Afterwards, they drove to the small strip mall where the sisters wandered around arm in arm, window-shopping and occasionally going inside one of the small stores. Razer and Shade sat on their bikes, keeping a close eye on the women. They came out of one shop with several bags, laughing before they then stopped when they saw the guys.

"What wrong?" Razer asked.

"How are we going to get the bags to campus?" Beth

asked in return.

As Razer and Shade split the load between them, stashing the bags of clothes into their saddlebags, one bag dropped and a waterfall of colorful underwear fell to the pavement.

"Oh." Lily immediately bent, hastily putting the clothes back inside the bag. One bright red pair fell by Shade's boot and, before Lily could pick it up, he had the silky material in his hands, slipping it into the bag she was holding.

Red as the underwear she had just purchased, Lily could only mutter her response. "Thanks."

"No problem." Shade's response was just as strangled.

Their shopping completed, they got back onto the bikes and returned to the small campus where the men got out Lily bags and said their goodbyes.

"Thank you for bringing, Beth. Goodbye." Beth walked Lily back to her dorm room, happy to see the color and life back in her eyes.

"I'll come down next Saturday to spend the day and night with you. How does that sound?"

"It's sounds wonderful. I'll see you then." With hugs and promises of phone calls, they also said their goodbyes. Beth left happily, certain that Lily would be fine until next weekend.

The ride back was relaxing as it was starting to get dark. Beth didn't worry with Razer guiding the bike across the opaque roads and she was almost sad the day had come to an end when they arrived back at the well-lit club. The house was filled again, but Beth and Razer were tired, going to their room. Shade, however, disappeared into the kitchen without a word.

Showering together, Razer and Beth languorously washed each other before grabbing towels. While Razer sprawled naked on the bed, he watched as she put on a t-shirt and a new purple thong. Brushing her hair, he caught a glimpse of her ass every time she lifted her hand to move the brush through her strands.

When she went to get in bed, Razer stopped her. "Come here, kitty, you are not done riding tonight."

"Razer, I'm a little sore from being on the bike. Can I just suck you off?"

Razer shook his head. "I had that pussy pressed against me all day and I want pussy tonight. You *are* going to give it to me." Arrogance poured out of him, but he was making her wet with his words. Beth crawled towards him, kissing his lips with tiny nips. Razer's hands swallowed her breasts, massaging them until she tried to fall back and pull him between her legs. Her body had become accustomed to having Razer several times a day; now all he had to do was look at her and it was torture. She simply wanted to feel the pleasure of his cock within her. Soreness be damned.

"No, kitty, I said you were going to ride." Still, when Beth tried to straddle him, he stopped her and faced her away from him, placing a leg on each side of his hips.

"I am going to see that pussy take all of me." His hands brought her down on his cock.

Beth began moving slowly up and down, sliding his full length deeper and deeper within her. She faced the door, which had a mirror on the back, giving Beth a view of what was happening on the bed. A hand at her back had her leaning forward, bracing her hands beside his knees as she continued to ride up and down his large member, helplessly watching the mirror.

"I can see all my kitty's cream this way. That tight little pussy stretching to take my cock." His fingers slid through the cream escaping her sheathe, rubbing his thumbs in it and slickening his fingers before moving them to her tiny rosebud.

"Are you a sweet little virgin here, too?" His thumb began to probe her ass. Startled, Beth almost jerked off him to move away from his touch, but a hard smack to her ass had her settling back down until once again his cock was deep within her.

"Bad kitty. Now be still." His thumb circled her rosebud again before he began inserting the thumb inside her, past her restricting muscles that were trying to keep him out.

"Fuck me harder," Razer ordered.

Beth's trembling body followed his commands as she once again found a rhythm that was bringing them the most pleasure. Tiny whimpers were escaping her at the feel of his thumb pushing into her ass in combination with the glide of his dick sliding in and out of her pussy. Her hands threatened to give out, yet she managed to maintain the position he wanted. When another thumb pushed in, stretching her hole, Beth's whimpers increased at the bite of pain.

"Now, that's a very good kitty," Razer crooned as his thumbs began a scissoring motion that had her trying to clench her ass. Her pussy was tightening around him and his hips had finally started to thrust upward, driving himself harder into her.

She had been slightly sore before they'd started having sex and, with the motions of his cock and his thumbs in her ass, the pain was adding to her stimulation, making her body move to capture it. The exquisite pain was as breathtaking as the orgasm she was desperately reaching for.

"You're going to have trouble walking tomorrow. Everyone's going to know I fucked you hard and long tonight." Razer's solid thrusts were driving her insane. "You ready to come?"

"Yes," Beth whimpered.

Razer pushed his thumbs deep into her ass and thrust up inside her pussy, hitting just the right spot to send her flying. Soft mewls were escaping her as he pulled his thumbs out, lifting her up and off his cock.

"Now, it's my turn." He slid out from under her and then flipped her to lie on her belly before he raised her hips, sliding a pillow under her pelvis. His sheathed cock slid in and out again, grinding into her until his balls were slapping against her flesh. Her fingers grabbed the bed sheets, holding on for dear life as his hands pulled her hips back against him, making sure he went as deep as possible. A series of hard thrusts later had him coming with Beth going over the edge once again, this time unable to prevent the screams that were torn from her throat.

Razer disposed of the condom and gently cleaned Beth. He then pulled her to him so that they were both lying on the rumpled bed, too hot to bear the covers on top of them. With their legs tangled, Razer's hand found his resting place on her breast.

"I can now see why it took two women to satisfy you," Beth said wearily. Razer didn't correct her misinformation. Sometimes, he could go through three or four, depending on how energetic or inventive he felt. Tonight, however, he was oddly content and satisfied with just Beth. Not wanting to think about it too closely, he closed his eyes and went to sleep, unconsciously trapping her with a lean leg thrown over hers.

CHAPTER FOURTEEN

Beth woke up mid-morning, regretting that she was unable to go to church again that Sunday. It was a habit she'd had for as long as she could remember and the church was a part of her life. She sighed as she gazed over to where Razer was sprawled on his stomach. Beth was tempted to wake him, but he had early shifts the coming week and she wanted him to catch up on his sleep.

She grabbed a quick shower, dressing in a pair of cut off jeans and an overlong t-shirt that had a cat playing with a ball of yarn. Smiling mischievously, she thought Razer would appreciate the humor. Closing the door behind her, she went downstairs to the kitchen where the aromas of coffee and bacon filled the air. Her stomach growled. She hadn't eaten since yesterday with Lily. With that thought in mind, Beth made a mental note to be sure that she saved Razer enough food because he would be even more starved than she was.

"Best night I ever freakin' had," Natasha was telling Jewell. "He was a fucking machine."

When the women saw Beth approaching, they changed the subject, talking about the chore board they had sitting in front of them. Beth tried not to let it bother her. She liked both girls and had thought they liked her also.

"What's for breakfast?" Beth smiled at both of them and walked to the counter to pour herself some coffee.

"There are some eggs and bacon left. Oh, and Evie made some awesome cinnamon rolls. They're in the oven."

Beth checked and saw that they had been put in there to be kept warm. Tearing one off the baking sheet, she went to the counter and sat down, sipping the coffee. The cinnamon roll melted in her mouth and, licking her lips, the sugar glaze dissolved against her tongue.

As she took another bite, warm arms slid around her waist and a hand in her hair pulled until her head fell back on Razer's shoulder. Lips fastened to hers, licking the sugar glaze that had clung to her lips.

"Mmm… delicious."

When Razer released her, Beth smiled at him as he went to the stove to fix a huge plate of food. Loading two of the huge cinnamon rolls on his plate.

"You're going to get fat the way you eat," Beth teased.

Razer's teeth picked up a crisp piece of bacon. "I plan to work off the calories after breakfast," he said with a wink.

"Nope, I have work to do. I am determined to finally get Mrs. Langley's boxes organized today. When you get done eating, could you get them for me?"

"Yes, I'll do it before going for a run," Razer said, biting into a cinnamon roll and giving her a sloppy kiss before leaving the room right as Evie came in looking like hell. Memphis and Crash, who were following behind her, didn't look much better.

"The cinnamon rolls are great, Evie."

"I fixed them before I went to bed." When Evie would take a mood to cook something, she did it regardless of the time. No one would know *when* the mood would strike, but they all benefited when it did. Beth got up, snagging another one before they all disappeared and poured herself another cup of coffee.

"I'm going upstairs to get busy. I want to organize Mrs. Langley's papers and give them back tomorrow when one of us does her house. I'll be back later when you're awake and we'll divide the schedule," Beth teased Evie.

"Take your time," Evie replied, smacking Memphis's hand before he could take three cinnamon rolls. "Damn people, there should have been enough to have some left over until tomorrow."

Smiling, Beth headed out of the kitchen, leaving the others amicably arguing. Precariously opening the door to Razer's room, she was careful not to spill the coffee. Setting it on the nightstand, she went to the boxes and set them in the middle of the floor. Opening the first one, she worked steadily, going through years of financial records that had been stored. She was surprised that Mrs. Langley's son-in-law had not shredded them because she didn't see anything of any importance. She put everything back and marked on the box for the papers to be shredded. She would check with Mrs. Langley before she took care of that task.

Taking a break, she finished her now cold coffee and cinnamon roll, debating about leaving some of it for later, but she was determined to finish the task. She used the restroom and sat back down, cross-legged on the floor once again.

Beth pulled the second box towards her, opening it. Beth stared at the papers, not sure what she was looking at. Then, with a sick feeling, she emptied the box and meticulously organized the papers until she could understand what she had found.

Afterwards, she carefully returned most of the papers to the box, closing the contents inside. Going to Razer's nightstand, she took the sheaf of papers she had not returned to the box and hid them inside a magazine in the drawer. She had just closed the drawer, picking up her cell phone to call the Sheriff, when she heard the door open.

Beth, thinking it was Razer, was not surprised, however, to see Sam standing with a gun pointed directly at her.

"I see you're not surprised to see me."

"I'm not." Beth clutched the phone in her hand.

"Put it down, Beth."

Beth could tell by the cold look in the young woman's eyes that she would kill her, so she laid the phone down on the nightstand.

"Sam, don't do this. You're not involved."

"Shut up. Pick up the box and let's go." Beth didn't argue, figuring her chances were better outside the room than enclosed within it along with Sam. Beth picked up the box and went out the door with Sam following close behind her.

"Everyone is in the backyard going over the work schedule. If you make a sound, I will shoot you."

Beth went down the steps, tempted to throw the box at her. "Don't do it, Beth, I will shoot you then take off before anyone comes. If not, then I will shoot whoever shows up."

Beth went through the door to the outside, truly frightened, not knowing what to do. Sam directed her to a low-slung, white sports car, ordering her to get inside. Keeping the gun pointed at her, she walked around to the other side of the car and got in. Sam started the powerful car, driving out of the lot, headed to town.

"Samantha, your father is not worth you going to prison for the rest of your life. The club will figure it out. They aren't stupid, they'll know someone from the house took me."

"I've already got that covered. No one will know it's me. And no, they won't figure out shit. They still don't know who killed Viper's brother. It took a stupid bitch like you to figure out my dad was responsible."

"Why were the papers in that box?"

"The stupid fucker hid them there. He had gone to my grandmother's to destroy them, but he got interrupted, so he stashed them. He was going to destroy them, but he figured they were safe where they were, not expecting that dumbass worker of yours to actually take the boxes. If my dad hadn't been such an arrogant bastard, he would have destroyed the papers. Lazy fuck."

Sam drove through town without stopping, heading toward the county line. Beth didn't recognize the house they pulled into as they travelled down a long unpaved driveway. Sam drove around the back and parked the car beside an expensive BMW.

"Stay here until I come around."

Beth followed her order as terror began to fill her. She was out in the middle of nowhere with no one even aware she was missing.

"Get the box."

"Sam—"

"Move bitch, don't make me tell you again."

Beth got out the car and walked towards the house with Sam still holding the gun to her back while following her. She slowly went up the short flight of steps, opening the door while juggling the box, to find Samantha's father waiting inside the small kitchen. He was sitting at with a gun lying on the table before him.

"It's about time," he snapped at Sam as soon as she walked through the doorway.

"I had to wait until it was clear," Sam explained

He got up from the table and took the box from Beth's hands. Setting it on the table, he opened the box and took out the papers on top. The deeper down he went, not finding what he wanted, the more enraged he became until he started tossing the papers out haphazardly. When the box was empty, he angrily threw it at Beth.

"You idiot, didn't you check to see if the documents were there?"

"I didn't have time. The box was closed when I went in the room. How was I supposed to know she was smart enough to take the papers out?"

"You check!" Vincent Bedford screamed at his daughter.

"I can go back and get the papers." Sam turned to Beth and smacked her across the face. "What did you do with them?"

Beth's hand touched her stinging cheek, refusing to answer.

"I will shoot your kneecap. I can look if I have to, but it will be quicker and less painful for you if you tell me where they are."

"I put them in the closet." Beth lied, hoping Razer would find her going through his closet and become suspicious.

"She's lying."

"No shit," Sam snapped back at her father. Furiously, she hit Beth again with the gun in her hand. Pain burst through Beth's jaw as she fell, barely managing to catch herself by grasping the end of the table. When her hand cupped her cheek, this time Beth felt wetness against her fingers.

"Now where are the fucking papers? This is the last time I am going to ask before I leave. If I search your room and someone comes in, I will shoot. Do you want to be responsible for someone being hurt?"

Beth tried to think what her best option was, but she was drawing a blank. She didn't want anyone hurt and Sam was determined to find the papers. She obviously had no compunction about hurting someone. Beth didn't want to endanger Razer, but Viper deserved to know what had happened to his brother as well as with the money that he and the other club members had invested. With her mind still racing for options, a rough hand in her hair jerked her toward Vincent Bedford.

"Tell me where you put the papers. I will put a bullet through your brain if you don't." Beth felt the cold metal of the gun he was holding press against her temple.

"I put them in a brown shoe box in the closet," Beth

lied again. It was the only choice she had. They were going to kill her anyway. Bedford wouldn't release her and let her identify him and Sam for kidnapping.

This time it was Vincent Bedford who slammed the gun into her head. Beth momentarily blacked out as he threw her to the dirty kitchen floor. Her vision was blurry as she fought for consciousness while crashing and screaming pounded through her head, but she couldn't focus enough to understand what was going on. Darkness was growing at the edges of her vision, threatening to take her under, but with a last ditch effort, she managed to turn her head to see Cash restraining Samantha, who was fighting like a wildcat trying to get away from him.

Loker James and Bedford were fighting, if it could even be called that. Loker had two knives, one in each hand, and was cutting Bedford to shreds. The older man was covered in blood and was trying to defend himself in vain.

Beth felt Razer's touch as he moved her tumbled hair from her face. She had never seen that look on Razer's face. He had always been easy going or humorous, however this man before her was a cold-blooded killer, furious that she had been hurt.

She managed to see that Loker was now playing with Bedford, letting him think he was going to get out the back door when he turned to flee, yet at the last moment, Loker kicked him in the back, forcing him to fall forward onto the floor. The man attempted to crawl away from the assaulter, but Loker stepped on his hand, stopping his forward momentum. The scream of agony had her wincing in sympathy, even though the man had threatened to kill her.

"Loker, stop," Beth said weakly.

He ignored her, bringing his boot back and Beth knew he was about to plant it in the wailing man's face.

"Please, Loker, stop. I have all the proof you need to convict him back at the clubhouse."

This time he stopped and looked at her.

"Cover him," Razer spoke to someone she couldn't see.

Razer brushed his thumb against her cheek. "You're all right, sweetheart. The ambulance is on the way."

"How did you find me?"

"Loker was watching Bedford and, when he saw Sam come in with you, he called us."

"I had to, he threatened to kill my baby. He gave me no choice." Sam hung pitifully in Cash's arms, all the fight drained out of her. "He paid someone to take my baby. I don't even know if it was a boy or girl. He took the baby while I was unconscious after the delivery. He won't tell me where my child is or even with whom." The whole room went quiet, listening to Sam's heart wrenching cries. "It was Gavin's child."

"You lying bitch," Loker yelled.

The sounds of the siren approaching made Beth's head ache, though when she tried to move her head, the attempt had stars bursting through her skull. The last thing she remembered was Loker's hand around Sam's throat.

"Razer," she whispered as darkness overwhelmed the pain.

CHAPTER FIFTEEN

The beeping of a machine woke her and, turning her head, she saw a nurse punching buttons on a machine.

"Awake at last. We were starting to get worried about you. I'll call the doctor and he'll be in to talk to you." Giving her hand an impersonal pat, the uniformed nurse left.

Beth looked around the small room, hoping no one had called Lily. She didn't want to worry her.

The door opened and a tall man with bright red hair came in. His friendly eyes soothed Beth's frayed nerves. "I'm glad to see that you've regained consciousness. How are you feeling?"

"Confused."

"That's normal. Do you remember what happened?"

Beth started to nod, but the sharp pain rushing through her skull stopped the motion.

"I remember Sam kidnapped me and her father threatened to kill me."

"They almost succeeded, you have a severe concussion. You have been unconscious for twelve hours."

"Did anyone notify my sister?"

"No, the Sheriff accepted responsibility. If you had

stayed unconscious much longer, then he would have. The Sheriff said you wouldn't want to worry her."

Beth gave a sigh of relief. "Thank you. My sister would have been terrified, I 'm glad you took the Sheriff's advice."

The doctor gave her reassurances that she would heal quickly and he would release her in forty-eight hours.

"We want to keep a strict eye on you to make sure you're all clear before we release you."

"Thank you." The doctor left, giving her instructions to let the nurse know if she experienced any changes in pain and then sleep beckoned once more. Beth dozed on and off throughout the day, only waking intermittently with the arrival of the dinner tray. She managed to eat a small amount, hoping it would help the sick feeling in her stomach; however she was already back asleep when the nurse returned to retrieve the tray.

* * *

The next day, Beth felt much clearer. She was stronger and even able to get out of bed with an aide's help to take a shower and shampoo her hair. Afterward, she put on a clean gown on and was drying her hair with a towel while sitting in the chair by the window overlooking the parking lot.

She had hoped Razer or Evie would have come to visit her, at least letting her know what had happened after she had passed out, but no one came until late afternoon when the Sheriff finally arrived.

"Hello, Sheriff," Beth greeted him when he didn't see her sitting in the bed.

His concerned frown disappeared and a relieved smile replaced it. "So, you're up and about already?"

"At least as far as this chair. I'm still a little dizzy if I move too fast, but it's getting better."

"Good." The sheriff came to stand beside her as he looked out the window. "Want to tell me what happened yesterday?" he asked.

Beth told him about looking through the boxes and ended with where she had hidden the incriminating papers.

"Did Razer find the papers?"

"Yes. He found them when he went back to his room. Sam told him what you had found and what they were. She told everything she knew in order to try to cut a deal for herself. Bedford kept telling her to shut up."

"He was going to kill me. Is he in jail?"

"No, he's in the hospital also. Pretty bad shape, but he'll live and stand trial for murder as well as your kidnapping."

"So, was it true that he took Sam's baby?"

"It looks like it. We have to wait for the evidence to come back to know without a doubt."

"Poor Samantha."

The Sheriff looked at her in amazement. "Poor Samantha? She kidnapped you, pistol whipped you, was going to let her father kill you, and you feel sorry for her?"

"Yes, you protect family. Always."

The sheriff shook his head at the woman sitting before him. He had never met another person like her. Her soul was filled with concern for others more than herself. She had always been like that, even as a younger girl. There was no one, male or female, that he respected more than her.

"At least I don't have to worry about someone trying to kill me now that the mystery is solved," she said, relieved.

The sheriff hesitated. "Yes, it's over. You can go back to your normal life."

A thought struck her, which would explain why Razer hadn't been to visit her. "Did Razer get in trouble for hurting Mr. Bedford? He was only trying to protect me… it was actually Loker James who beat him so badly."

The Sheriff held up his hand, stopping her explanation. "I didn't arrest him, or James, either. The way I wrote it down was self-defense. Cash backed his story up."

"Oh… well, that's a relief." Beth bit her lip.

"The doctor said you'll be released tomorrow. My wife plans to come by and help you out until you feel better."

"No, I'll be fine—"

"You know Rachel won't take no for an answer, so no use in arguing. I brought your car to you. It's in the lot." Taking the keys out of his pocket, he handed them to her. "Rachel said to tell you she'd give you a few hours peace before she comes by."

"Thanks, Sheriff. I appreciate all your help."

"Anytime, Beth."

The sheriff stayed until the nurse came in to take her vitals, but Beth barely paid attention to the nurse's questions. She had been stunned when the Sheriff had handed her the keys to her car. It had been parked at the clubhouse. Razer would have to have given him the keys. Yet, he had sent no messages, nor had Evie. Beth tried hard not to be hurt, yet she couldn't help feeling ignored by the people she had come to care about.

CHAPTER SIXTEEN

Beth was released the next day after the doctor gave her a final exam. Feeling much better, she happily signed her release papers. Once outside, she had no trouble locating her car. Beth came to a decision as she drove home. She was going to find out why no one had come by the hospital to check on her, why no one had even called.

All the way there, Beth tried to talk herself out of her decision. A feeling of foreboding came over her, reminding her that she should go home, but for once, she didn't listen to the reasonable voice in her head that said to give it a couple of days.

When she pulled up to the house, the yard and porch were filled with bikers, none of them she recognized. As she walked to the front door, she was given many curious looks, but no one said anything to her.

Walking into the house she saw Razer immediately, Bliss was sitting on his lap with a black pair of leather shorts and a black vest completely open baring her breasts. Razer was sitting and playing with her nipple.

Once upon a time, Beth would have turned and ran away, unable to face the pain of jealousy that seeing him with another woman would evoke. Evie, who was sitting on Crash's lap, was the first to see her and her mouth dropped open before a carefully closed expression came over her face.

Razer turned to see what had startled Evie and also saw Beth. He didn't remove his hand, but the smile he'd been sporting disappeared in a flash.

Beth felt her legs carrying her across the room to stand before him. "Hi, Razer, Evie. I thought I would stop by and see if everyone was all right. I'd hoped you would come by the hospital to see me." Beth's voice was hesitant as she deliberately kept her eyes on Razer's face while his hands stroked Bliss's breasts.

"Didn't need to; the Sheriff told us you were fine." Razer gave a negligent shrug. "Since we found out who was responsible for stealing the money, we can open the factory. The other members came in from Ohio, so we've been busy celebrating."

"I see that."

"Actually, I'm glad you showed up." Evie got up from Crash's lap and opened the closet, dragging out Beth's suitcase and a large canvas bag. Bringing both to Beth, she continued, "I was going to bring this down to your house later today. Since the factory is going to open full-time, I don't need the extra work. My folders and keys are in the bag. Crash, could you take these to Beth's car for her?"

Crash rose from the chair, picking up the suitcase and the bag before leaving the room. His look screamed that he was glad to escape the upcoming confrontation. Beth wanted to flee as well so that she could keep her pride intact, however she was determined to see it through to the bitter end.

"Can I talk to you in private for a few minutes?" she asked Razer.

"There's no need. Look, there is no reason to make this hard, Beth. I let you crash here while there was a hit out on you, but now it's over. We both had a good time, but I kinda need my room and my space back." His hand dropped to delve between Bliss's thighs. Her head fell back to his shoulder and her thighs spread wider.

Beth closed her eyes. "Please, Razer, I can…" Her voice trailed off as her pleading blue eyes stared into his emotionless ones.

"Listen, bitch, I don't know how much more blunt I have to be, but here goes. We had fun, but I don't want or need a permanent roommate. I like variety in my pussy, and I can see by the way you look at me that you're getting too attached. I don't want attachments. What I do want— again—is pussy. I offered you a place to stay that was safe while you needed it, you don't need it anymore. The bad guy is in jail, so you're safe. You can go home and I can have my room back."

Razer stood up, holding Bliss who wrapped her legs tightly around his waist. "Now, if you'll excuse us, I'm going to my room to see if her pussy is as tight as yours was when I popped your cherry." With those last cutting words, Razer gave her his back, carrying a clinging Bliss up the stairs with him.

Beth stood there a few seconds after she heard his door close, forcing the nausea in her throat down. After several deep breaths, she pasted a fake smile on her face and left the house with everyone in the room a witness to her humiliation. In her car, she started it aware of several eyes watching her from the house, but she ignored them and carefully drove home.

Beth didn't remember the drive, only realizing where she was when she sat down on the couch. She wasn't sure how long she sat there before a knock brought her back to awareness. Automatically, she answered the door to find the Sheriff's wife outside.

"Beth, you look horrible. I can't believe they released you so soon. If I had realized you looked so bad, I would've been here immediately."

"I'm fine. I just ran an errand before I came home and ended up overdoing it. As soon as I get some rest, I'll be good as new."

The woman's sharp gaze studied her for several seconds before ushering her upstairs to bed, helping her to shower and then putting her to bed like a child. Pulling the covers over her, she even leaned down and brushed a small kiss on Beth's bruised cheek.

"Don't worry, dear, everything always looks better the next day." Rachel turned the lights out, reminding her just to call out if she needed anything, since she was staying the night in Lily's room. Beth wanted to argue with her, but exhaustion and heartache stopped her. She was too tired to put up an argument.

CHAPTER SEVENTEEN

Rachel was wrong, everything was not better the next day. Beth dragged herself out of bed early, determined to get back to work. Her clients depended on her and she was not going to let them down. The sheriff's wife argued with her about going back to work so soon, however Beth was firm in her insistence that she was better. Finally, the good-hearted woman left her in peace, saying she would call her that evening.

Beth made her rounds of clients. It was hard to get all the patients done since Evie had quit and she was literally shaking by the time she let herself into her house where she immediately collapsed on the sofa.

Curling into a ball, she snagged the phone, calling Rachel to tell her she was going to bed and would not need her assistance that night. Hearing the hurt in the woman's voice, Beth almost broke, but she hardened her resolve and said goodnight. Beth fell asleep for several hours, waking to fix herself some soup, which she ate with no appetite, yet she knew she had to eat to keep her strength.

The last two days of the week were more of the same. Beth worked hard and ate what she could force down her throat. All the time aware her heart was breaking.

Imagining Razer with the different women at the clubhouse was like a movie playing in her mind. The picture of Razer stroking Bliss was engraved in her memory and it tormented her constantly.

On Saturday, she drove to see Lily. Her sister took one look at her bruised face and heartbroken eyes and simply held her arms open. Beth and Lily lay on her tiny bed as she was finally able to let go, crying her misery onto her sister's shoulder. Lily lay next to her, stroking her back as she murmured questions, giving her unconditional love to soothe her broken ego.

"I hate him," Beth sobbed.

"I do, too," Lily whispered her agreement.

"I miss him so badly. I don't think I can do this, Lily. Maybe if I go talk to him?"

"Do you think it would matter to him?"

"No."

"Then that answers your question."

"I love him, Lily."

"I know, but you can't have him. You have to let it go."

"I don't know if I can," Beth admitted, ashamed of being so weak.

"Then let's go." Lily stood up. "We can leave now and be there in a couple of hours." Beth also got up and picked up her keys along with her purse. She actually made it to the door before she stopped. Her forehead touched the door as she started crying again. She didn't resist when Lily led her back to sit on the bed.

"It's over."

"Yes, Beth, whatever you shared with Razer is over." With those words, Beth accepted what she had known from the first time she had seen Razer in front of the police station with that motorcycle; that given half a chance, he would break her heart.

CHAPTER EIGHTEEN

The party was dying down and the ones who hadn't been lucky enough to find a bed for the night were sprawled on any available furniture sturdy enough to hold their weight. Several had even thought ahead, bringing a sleeping bag and finding an open piece of floor to crash on.

Slowly, methodically, he went down the steps, careful, not to make a sound. He didn't want to wake anyone. He had planned everything down to the final detail, determined no drunk-assed member would screw his plans up at the last minute.

With his thumb on the detonator, he headed for the door. The sudden burst of light coming on blinded him for a second. Startled, he spun around to see Viper, Razer and Cash standing by the door.

"Hey man, you're going to wake everyone. Douse the lights."

"Everyone is already awake. What are you doing awake? Last I saw, you were upstairs with Evie."

Memphis shrugged. "She's asleep. I thought I'd go for a ride."

"Sounds good; care if we join you?" Viper asked.

"I was wanting some alone time, if you don't mind?" Memphis started to move forward, but the three men blocked his path.

"We do mind."

Memphis turned to leave through the backdoor, but found his way blocked by the members he thought had been sleeping. Outnumbered, he tried to brazen his way out.

"What's up, Viper? Since when does me going for a ride become club business?"

"It becomes our business when you're planning on blowing us to smithereens on your lone ride."

"I don't know what the fuck you're talking about."

"Search him, Razer," Viper ordered.

When Razer took a step forward, Memphis tried to make a break for it, trying to force himself through the men blocking the door, but he instantly found himself with his face shoved into the wall and his arms held high behind his back. When he tried to fight free, Viper smashed his face into the wall using his hair.

"Stay the fuck still."

Memphis felt hands going through his pockets. "Well, look what I found." Cash pulled the detonator out of his pocket, lifting it where all the members could see it. Razer jerked Memphis from the wall, throwing him across the room. Knox caught him, throwing him down on the couch.

"It took three fucking years of my life to figure out who betrayed my brother. You sorry piece of shit, you killed him for fifty grand. I would have given you the fucking money if you had asked, you motherfucker."

Memphis was aware that he was a dead man, so he also knew that lying would only make it more painful. "I would have done it for free." Memphis shrugged while Viper lunged at him, but Razer and Cash held him back.

"He's just trying to piss you off so you'll kill him quick. Find out your answers first," Razer reasoned.

"First, answer my question then I'll answer yours. How did you finally figure it out?" Memphis questioned.

"Sam, we promised protection and no jail time if she told us who her father paid to kill my brother," Viper answered.

"She didn't know. Bedford swore he wouldn't tell. He was scared enough of me to keep his mouth shut."

"Sam followed her father to one of your meetings. She recognized you when she started hanging around the house."

"Damn slut," Memphis muttered.

"I answered your question, now answer ours. "

"I killed Gavin because he was a pain in my ass. I was dealing drugs on the side and he was going to tell you at the next meeting. I would have been out. I couldn't have that going down. I had a plan and was going to stick to it no matter what happened. Him being dead distracted everyone enough that I was able to move a lot of the patents to my name and, with the money I made off them, as well as the insurance policy on everyone, I would have been a rich man."

The insurance policy had been taken out between the eight friends when they had started their survival business. That way, if any one was killed, the business would not be affected because the insurance was made out to the surviving group members. The bomb he had planted and planned to detonate would have killed a large number of them, especially those carrying the larger chunks of stock.

"What did you do with my brother's body?" Viper braced himself for Memphis's answer.

"I buried him behind the Road Demon's clubhouse." That time, when Viper struck out at Memphis, no one tried to stop him. He pulled back and landed a final jab to his jaw, which sent Memphis down to the floor, groaning and curling into a ball.

"Tomorrow, I'll ask for a meet with the Road Demon's to try and get Gavin's body. If it's not there—"

"I'm telling the truth. What are you going to do with me?"

"Keep you alive long enough to bring Gavin home. After that, the club will deal with you one by one."

Memphis had hoped for a quick death, but Viper had taken away that prospect with his words. Each of the original members would stand in a circle with him positioned in the middle, the members would then each have the opportunity to give him a killing blow. It wouldn't matter if he were dead after the one chosen to go first. In this case, because it was Viper's brother, he would be allowed the first strike. After each had their turn, he would be disposed of just as he had disposed of Gavin. The only difference was Gavin would now be coming home to a proper burial.

"We're going to show you the same mercy that you showed my brother." Viper's promise was deadly accurate.

CHAPTER NINETEEN

Beth came out of the restaurant, her heels clicking on the pavement. Pastor Dean had asked to meet her to talk. It had been hard sitting at the booth with him since it brought back memories of the dates they had shared, interchanged with thoughts of what might have happened if she hadn't been so attracted to Razer from the moment she'd seen him. Fortunately, Beth had realized that a relationship with Dean would have never worked. The sexual chemistry that she'd shared with Razer was absent with Dean.

The meeting hadn't lasted long. He was unhappy with the way she was looking, and Beth had to admit that she had lost quite a bit of weight since Razer had finished with her. The paleness of her face and her lackluster hair gave her an appearance of being ill.

"Thank you for your concern, but I am fine." Beth laid her hand on top of his, seeing the disbelief in his eyes. "It's not every day a girl gets kidnapped and pistol whipped." She gave a self-deprecating smile. "Perhaps I should have taken that Las Vegas trip." Beth had returned his gift, not wanting to go alone. She had no one that she could bear to spend time with right now other than Lily and she was

179

busy with school.

"I could still arrange it for you."

"No, thank you. I have no one to cover my patients right now. Perhaps this summer when Lily is out of school. I have a couple of interviews next week to hire someone to replace Evie." Dean saw the flash of pain that Beth was unable to hide. Without hesitating, though, Beth began discussing church business, offering to volunteer to have a rummage sale for a member who had a fire which had destroyed their belongings.

Dean leaned back in his seat, watching her pick at her food as she talked, getting the message that the members of The Last Riders were not up for discussion. Not long after, Beth left Dean sitting with two church members who had stopped by their table to volunteer their services. With a grin, she escaped, using the excuse of an early workday.

Outside, it was just getting dark when she heard the loud motors of the bikes. Beth didn't hesitate in her footsteps across the parking lot, neither did she turn her head to see the passing bikers. It was only when she almost walked into Razer's bike that she lifted her head. Another pulled in behind her, pinning her between the two bikes. Shade and Evie each gave her a nod as Razer and Shade's motors were cut. The sudden silence was a relief.

"Beth."

"Razer."

"How have you been?"

"Good." Beth didn't ask how he was, she didn't care. At least that was what she kept telling herself.

"You don't look so good."

Beth shrugged. "Appearances can be deceiving." Razer nodded while Beth stared at her car behind his back to keep from looking at him.

Razer cleared his throat, drawing her attention to him. Beth glared at his mirrored sunglasses to keep from having to look at him on his bike. His hair was a little longer since the last time she'd seen him. Wearing leather pants and a black shirt with a leather jacket, she wanted to jump on the back of his bike and forget everything that had happened. A wry smile touched her lips at imagining Razer's horrified reaction if she did.

"Yes, they can. That's why I want to talk to you. Can we go somewhere to talk? I would like to explain some things to you."

"No explanations are necessary, you got your message across clearly the last time I saw you." Beth took a step to the right, trying to get to her car.

"Beth, let him explain. I want to tell you how sorry I am for the way things went down. If you would listen…" Evie trailed off as Beth stopped and turned, meeting her eyes. Evie flinched from the pain that Beth didn't try to hide this time.

"I don't need explanations, Evie. I provided employment for you until the factory opened. It's not your fault that I misinterpreted it and thought we had become friends."

"We were friends… no, we are friends. Beth, listen to me—"

With a sad smile, Beth shook her head as she spoke over Evie once again, "No, Evie, you are no friend of mine. You left me in that hospital to wake up alone, scared and not knowing what had happened. I kept thinking you would come by and bring me a few magazines or couple of things I could have used. You never did, though. Then, when I came to the club and was humiliated in front of everyone by a man I cared about, did my friend stand by me? No. She ignored me and cut me deep by quitting when I needed her the most. Did my friend come by and see me to let me cry on her shoulder? No, you didn't. A friend would have been there for me. I would have been there for you." When Beth finished in a soft voice, Evie looked stricken. Again Beth took a step, determined to leave.

"Beth, wait… I can explain." Razer's hand snapped out and caught her arm, keeping her from leaving.

Beth took a deep breath and let Razer have his piece also. "Razer, explanations are not necessary for the simple reason that they won't make a difference to how I feel about you. You were wrong that night at your house. I wasn't beginning to care for you, I had fallen in love with you. I knew you didn't return my feelings and I let it happen anyway. I've had a few bad weeks since then, but I am getting over you. If the explanations you want to give me end with you wanting to be friends, that won't work for me. It would be too painful for me to see you with other women and not touch you myself." When Razer would have spoken, Beth raised a hand to stop him. "Let me finish. On the other hand, if you are hoping these explanations lead to us being back together again, that no longer is an option. You are incapable of giving me the relationship I need to be happy, which involves trust, fidelity and love. Even if you swore to do all three, I would never, ever believe in you again."

This time, when Beth took a step forward, Razer's hand dropped to his side. Both bikes sat immobile as Beth carefully maneuvered her SUV around them, pulling out onto the road without a look backward.

* * *

"We fucked up bad." Evie's head fell forward to Shade's back.

"More like crashed and burned," Dean said, stepping out from behind a parked van.

"Back off, Dean. You had no business eavesdropping."

"I had every right. I handed you that girl on a silver platter, and what did you do? You screwed her over so badly that now, not only don't I have her, but you don't have her and it's not looking like you ever will." Dean ruthlessly threw Beth's words back in Razer's face.

"She'll come around; she'll forgive me. The girl is incapable of holding a grudge."

"Did you even make an attempt to get to know her?" Dean asked in disbelief.

"What does that mean?"

"It means, she is not going to forgive you. You hurt her too badly; she won't put herself back in that vulnerable position again, with either of you." The sympathy in Dean's voice had Razer feeling fear that he wouldn't get Beth back once he explained for the first time. He had never doubted that once she understood why he had broken it off with her, they would resume where they'd left off. Now, by the look in Deans eye, he felt he had overestimated the ability of Beth to forgive, if not forget.

"Come with me." Dean left the parking lot without another word, walking towards the church across the street.

"You two go on back to the club." Shade nodded and left with Evie at his back.

Razer rode his bike across the street, parking it before going inside the church to find Dean waiting in his office. There was a filing cabinet there and he was taking a key out to unlock it when Razer walked in.

Razer watched as he took out a medium-sized box and handed it to Razer. "Go home and watch a couple of these. When you're done, destroy them. I could only stomach watching a couple of them, but I think you need to see what you're up against."

"Why are you helping me? You already paid your favor back to me."

"This isn't about you, Razer. This is about a pastor doing what is best for a member of his congregation whom he put into harm's way." Razer took the words like a punch in the stomach. It was evident that Dean felt as if he had hurt Beth by giving Razer a chance with her.

Razer left without a word, strapping the heavy box onto the back of his bike, he headed to the clubhouse. Once there, he searched for a private room with a television, the box in his hands. Finding none, he ended up in the back room, which was empty, and hooked up the VCR recorder that Dean had also given him. Opening the box, Razer found each tape neatly dated along with the title of the sermon that Beth's father must have taped. Razer started at the earliest date.

Hitting play, Razer took a seat on the couch and watched as the grainy film came to life. A tall, thin man with wire-framed glasses stood behind the pulpit, giving a sermon. It was a thing to shrink a grown man's balls with hell and damnation used as threats. He gave a blistering sermon that would have put the fear of God into a grown man, much less the tiny girl sitting on the front pew by a rigidly stern woman who nodded her head in agreement with every sentence the preacher mouthed.

Razer recognized Beth immediately and a smile touched his lips at seeing her sitting so quiet and still throughout the longwinded sermon. Not that Razer listened; he fast forwarded through much of it and was about to stop it when a movement from Beth's father caught his eye, so he pressed play once again. He was motioning Beth to stand in front of the large congregation.

"Now, we come to the part of service where I give everyone a chance to repent their sins and take their punishment to be forgiven of them. My daughter will begin. Beth?"

Beth stared straight ahead as she stood before the congregation. Razer's gut clenched, it was the same look she had given him earlier that night

"I am pleading for forgiveness from my Lord to forgive my tardiness to dinner twice this week. My mother works hard to make the meal and my father works hard to provide it. I should be more appreciative and show my respect by being on time."

"Beth, do you repent your sins?"

"Yes, Pastor Saul."

"Then kneel before your peers and take your punishment."

Beth got to her knees as her father stood behind her carrying a leather strap.

"REPENT!" he screamed and the strap struck out, hitting the girl on her back.

The church members yelled back. "Repent."

Three more times the leather struck her on her back before her father allowed her to resume her seat. Horrified, Razer was unaware of Shade and Evie entering the room to stand behind the couch, watching. Clumsily, Razer removed the tape and put in the next one. He watched six more tapes, each with Beth getting strapped for little or no reason. Razer noticed not a single member of the congregation volunteered to repent their sins along with the child, yet each sat mindlessly as Beth took beating after beating. The room began to fill as member after member came to get dinner, becoming engrossed in the tapes being played. Razer continued to pay no notice to the fact that he was no longer alone.

Cash was one of the last ones to come in and he stood shakily behind the couch as one particular tape began. He remembered it well. In fact, he still had nightmares because of it. He had done two tours with the seals and no single sight had affected him as much as the tape brought back to life.

It wasn't a regular church meeting; instead, it seemed as if they were in a smaller church and the parishioners were standing around chanting. Razer didn't know what they were doing or saying as they danced in place and chanted in a language he had never heard before.

A large, bearded man went behind the podium and pulled out a snake. Beth who had been stepping slowly back and forth between her parents was pushed forward as the snake was held out. She didn't speak, she simply continued moving, holding out her frail, little arms. The snake slid up her forearm as, pale and obviously frightened, she couldn't have been more than nine-years-old. A look of pain and a whimper escaped her as the snake reared back and struck her in the upper arm.

"Praise God." The man pried the snake's teeth from her arm and she fell to the floor, crying as the parishioners circled around the whimpering child. Suddenly the tape ended as if the machine taping it had fallen to the floor.

"I remember that day. I tried to get to her and knocked the camera over."

"What the hell was that?" Jewell said in shock.

"Snake handling. Her bastard of a father would take us into the mountains once a year to a sister church. Every year I watched the same scene. Didn't Beth tell you when you saw the scars on her arms?"

"No." Disgust was eating at Razer that he hadn't tried to get to know Beth; that he had never even noticed the scars which marred her beautiful body.

"Did they take her to the hospital? Why didn't someone call social services?" Bliss questioned.

"No, they never took her to the hospital. The proof of faith is when she doesn't die. So no medical treatment, no one reported it to social services, and the Sheriff back then was a member of the congregation who couldn't have given a shit. The congregation prayed over her all night while her little body was wracked with pain till morning. It was the last time I ever prayed."

"The next year they went, they didn't make her do it again, did they?" Viper asked.

"As far as I know, from what my grandmother told me, yes. A couple of times it was a close call, but she survived. The members took it as a sign of their faith, but I would say it was more likely that she built up an immunity to the venom. I wouldn't know; I left town the next day and enlisted in the Navy. I never went back to that church."

Knowing now that he wasn't alone, Razer still went to the next box and picked a tape from a couple years later. He couldn't stop himself even if he'd wanted to; the desire to know more was overruling every other piece of common sense in his head. Beth would be about eleven, he thought. It was more of the same except the beating became worse. However, Razer noticed one deviation; she begged God's forgiveness, never her stern faced father, no matter how many times the leather struck her back.

The next tape had Lily's first appearance. The small, underweight child was brought forward as they explained the charity they'd had to give to a child in desperate need of a home. No mention was made of where she'd come from, though. Several tapes were gone through before the minister ordered Lily forward for a misdemeanor for punishment. When she would have stepped forward, Beth pulled her back, explaining it was her fault that Lily had committed what had been deemed as sin. The pastor, thwarted in his desire for new prey, took it out on a blank-faced Beth. This continued on until a tape where the pastor ordered Lily forward and when Beth would have stepped forward she was denied.

"You will sit, Beth. Lily will take the punishment for letting you influence her and then I will punish you for your part in it. It is time that Lily learned not to let you force her from the path of righteousness."

The strange part was that Lily didn't look frightened. A look of peace had come over her as she clasped her hands in front of her. Her silky, black hair fell forward as she repented in a strong voice. When the leather struck her, she didn't flinch or move; her voice remained the same monotone as before.

"I am going to throw up," Natasha warned.

Shade walked forward and jerked the tape out of the VCR before then throwing it at the television, which burst with sparks flying and not one member chastised him for doing so.

"Did that shit continue until the bastard got killed?" Razer asked Cash.

"No, by then the new sheriff was in town and, from what my grandmother wrote me, he had heard of what was going on, but no one would talk. Beth and Lily were home schooled, so he couldn't get the girls alone to talk to them, either. It wasn't long after he was appointed that Beth disappeared for an afternoon. When her parents searched for her, they found her at the restaurant across from the Sheriff where she was sitting, eating a sundae. Granny wrote she was frightened for Beth that following Sunday until the new Sherriff showed up before church and had a talk with Pastor Saul. After that, the Sheriff was there every church meeting, rain or shine. The girls both entered school the next school year, too."

"The sheriff probably threatened them with social services," Bliss guessed.

Cash gave an evil grin. "Bet he threatened to kill him if he touched them again."

"She won't forgive me, not after what I did. I humiliated her in front of everyone, just like he did. She was hurt and I ignored her just as those people stood around and didn't do a damn thing." His hands clenched into fists. "She begged me to talk to her in private…" Razer couldn't continue.

The women's smothered sobs could be heard in the silence of the room while the men moved to stand by their brother who sat staring sightlessly at a broken television with no hope in his heart that he would get the girl. They did what they always did, though, and supported their brother as they also came up with a plan of action. Because this mission was a rescue long over-do.

CHAPTER TWENTY

The week ended up becoming a nightmare for Beth. Her clients seemed to be abnormally demanding and, by the weekend, she was worn out. As she drove home, she refused to let herself think of Razer and the customary Friday night gathering at his house.

When she got home, she showered, but found herself antsy and couldn't settle down. Determined to get Razer and his activities out of her mind, she texted the girls she had met at the gas station on the way to visit Lily.

She'd been surprised when they'd first texted her and the conversation had been stilted. Several times she had wondered if they were trying to get information out of her about The Last Riders, but when she hadn't responded to their questions, the conservations had turned to girl talk. The women were as bored with their lives as she was with hers.

They had met up a couple of times, going to the movies or out to dinner. Both times Beth had driven to their town. Tonight they were coming to Treepoint and they were going to meet up at the Pink Slipper, a nightclub on the outskirts of town. It was the direct opposite of Mick's, with regular guys wanting to hook up. Beth had never been there before, however her new friends had wanted to celebrate Sex Piston opening her own beauty salon, so she'd given in.

Beth dressed in a black dress with a plunging neckline that complemented her full breasts. The dress came to below her knees, but the silky feel made her feel seductive. She slipped on her black heels, some jewelry, and was almost out the door when she turned back to change her shoes to dark purple high heels. Now, feeling as if she was going out to have fun instead of a funeral, Beth left to meet her friends.

She waited at the door for the girls to show up, and after about fifteen minutes, a bright green, four-door Chevrolet parked and out they came, dressed like biker bitches. With the leather skirts or pants cupping their asses and black t-shirts showing pert breasts, they made Beth feel old and ready to retire.

"Hey, girl. Been waiting long? We would have been here sooner, but T.A. had to stop for a piss."

"Don't blame me, you drive like my grandma." With that start, the good-hearted ribbing continued until long after they were seated at a large table.

"Okay, let's order some drinks and get the party started." Killyama ordered the waitress to bring drinks then sat back, proceeding to flirt shamelessly with a good-looking blond man at the bar.

"We plan on getting shit-faced and crashing at your place. You cool with that?" Crazy Bitch asked.

Beth smiled. "Yes, it'll be fun. We can have a girl's night."

Crazy Bitch just stared at her. "Girl, I didn't sneak away from my old man for a girl's night. I plan to find a man who can give me an actual orgasm."

Beth deflated. She didn't know how she felt about her house being used as a place for the women's hook-ups. "My house isn't very large."

"Got a spare bedroom?"

"My sister's room."

"She there?"

"No."

"Then it's all good. We can take turns using the room," Crazy Bitch announced.

Beth took a sip of the drink the waitress sat before her and decided to hope for the best. Maybe the women would strike out, but if they didn't, she would redo Lily's room and buy her a new mattress. Beth was beginning to see that the night wasn't going to be as worry-free as she had hoped.

This thought was further proven a few minutes later when she was casually studying the other patrons of the bar and her eyes met Winter Simmons's. Her mother was one of her former clients, who'd had breast cancer and, after a long, fierce battle, she had passed away the year before. Winter was as prim and proper as the Sunday school teacher she was; she also was the principal at the local high school. Her table was filled with two members of the PTA and Beth was curious as to why they would be in a nightclub at this time of night.

Crazy Bitch interrupted her train of thought, though, as she let out a whoop, whoop when a good-looking man asked Killyama to dance. Beth wanted to slide to the floor, yet brazened it out, smiling at Winter before turning her attention back to the women at her own table.

"So when is the big opening?"

"Monday. You going to come down and let me do your hair?"

"What's wrong with my hair?"

"Nothing." Her tone belied her words. "I just can make it better. You know, sexier, like ours." Beth stared at their teased and tortured hair which looked much different than the first time she had met them.

"I'm busy next week. I haven't hired anyone yet to replace Evie. I've set up several interviews that I'll have to fit in also. Hopefully one of them will work out and will be able to start immediately."

Sex Piston shrugged. "You got scissors at your house?"

Beth knew where this was going and tried to nip it in the bud. "No."

Sex Piston took a large sip of her drink. "That's okay. I'll stop at a convenience store and buy a pair."

Beth knew when she was beat. "I'll call Monday and make an appointment." A sober Sex Piston working on her hair was better than a drunk Sex Piston.

"That's my girl."

Beth watched as one by one, the women were asked to dance. Even Beth was surprised to be asked and was just returning from a rigorous two step when she looked at the doorway and experienced déjà vu. The difference this time was that it wasn't Razer's motorcycle club that had crashed the party, but the Destructors.

Beth heard Crazy Bitch, who was sitting next to her, mutter, "This is not going to be good."

Beth swallowed a large sip of her own drink while, for the first time, getting a good look at the rough bikers and agreed wholeheartedly.

CHAPTER TWENTY-ONE

Razer was going up to his room alone, the night was early, but he was in no mood to party. Not that the others were in much of a mood, either. The members were mainly playing pool or watching a new release on the television Shade had brought home that afternoon.

His cell phone ringing stopped him mid-step.

"Razer."

"Razer, this is Mick. You home?"

"Yeah. Why?"

"Thought you would want to know we got a couple guys in here that were in The Pink Slipper. They left because some bikers came in and started arguing with their bitches."

"Why would I care? We don't want a turf war over The Pink Slipper. They can have that pussy bar."

"I didn't think you would be concerned over turf. I thought you might be concerned that your woman was sitting in the middle of it."

"I don't…" Razer started to say he didn't have a woman before realization dawned on him. "Beth is there?"

"That's what I'm saying. She was there with the bitches and the men rolled in an hour later. Sound familiar?"

"It's a fucking set-up."

"Yeah."

Razer hung up on Mick, going back down the steps. The members in the room watched curiously as he went to the closet and pulled on the club's leather jacket.

"Going somewhere?" Shade asked

"Going to The Pink Slipper."

"What the fuck for?"

"To get something that belongs to me," he answered grimly, putting on his leather gloves. The other members stood and started getting ready as well. They weren't sure exactly what was going on, but they never let a brother go into what obviously was going to be some kind of battle alone.

Razer took the lead with thirty club members at his back when he turned into the bar to find just as many bikes already parked. When he and his brothers walked in, it didn't take long for him to locate Beth. She was sitting at a large table with four biker chicks sitting close to her while the rest of the table and chairs were filled with bikers; others stood blocking the table. Beth couldn't hide her frightened expression as the other women were arguing with the men.

Razer, with Viper, Shade, Cash, Knox and Rider at his side moved to the table. The rest of The Last Riders followed behind. Half of the patrons at the bar started motioning the waitress for their bills, the other half were raking cash out of purses and wallets, throwing it down on the table without waiting for their tickets. The menace coming from both groups of bikers was giving lethal vibes to the entire bar.

Beth's eyes widened when she saw the approaching menace-filled Razer. "Beth."

"Razer?"

"Let's go."

"Bitch isn't going nowhere with you or your men. Y'all need to get back on your machines and leave us to our fun," a bitch with her hair teased and crazy eyes answered for Beth.

"Beth, let's go. I'm not telling you again."

Beth's eyes narrowed in anger. "You don't have the right to tell me shit. Crazy Bitch is right, you guys need to leave us alone. We were minding our own business until everyone interfered."

"Minding what was in the pants of those pussies you bitches were dancing with when we showed up is more like it." Razer didn't recognize the man speaking from the gas station, but he figured that, from the way the guy talked and acted, he was the leader.

"Yeah, I don't care what you think, Ace. We came to celebrate my shop opening Monday. The same one you, or any of you assholes, didn't want to help paint or do shit to help with. I don't want you guys here tonight; you don't deserve to be part of our party."

"I didn't see that douche bag whose throat you had your tongue down doing any hammering there, either."

"Yeah, well, he was going to do plenty later tonight," Sex Piston taunted.

"Was he, or were they?" He jerked his head towards Razer's club. "Did you plan on hitting their clubhouse next?" Ace asked in a menace-laden voice.

"You kidding me? We were going to fuck around, not betray the club. If we were going to do that, we would have picked one worth the punishment of breaking a rule."

"Did she just put us down?" Knox asked.

"Yes, she did, dumbass," Sex Piston mocked.

Evie, Dawn, Jewell and Natasha pushed to the front of the men, standing by their club members.

"What the fuck are you doing here?" Viper questioned.

"Loker James?" Beth questioned, not sure the man standing beside Razer was indeed Ton's son. He bore no resemblance, even his facial features, which were the same, had changed. His already hardened features were an expressionless mask. He wasn't wearing a suit; instead he was clad in tight, leather pants, boots and a t-shirt with a leather vest.

A gasp from a nearby table had everyone turning to Winter Simmons's table where she was sitting with the PTA, avidly listening to every word being spoken.

"He's Viper," Evie explained. Now that Vincent Bedford had been arrested and Memphis dealt with, there was no longer any need to hide his identity.

Beth sat without knowing what to think while also remaining completely oblivious to the menace radiating back and forth between the two motorcycle groups.

"Well, that's none of my business, is it?" Beth said, picking up her drink with a trembling hand.

"To answer your question, if Beth was in trouble, we were going to be here to help," Evie answered Viper's question and ignored Beth's.

"Who the fuck are you?" Killyama asked.

"Evie," she answered in her toughest voice.

"You're the bitch who left Beth high and dry! Damn, girl, you got balls to stand there after you fucked her man then watched her man fuck these other bitches."

The other club was beginning to look at The Last Rider's members with dawning respect.

"How d'you manage that, man? My bitch would cut my balls off in my sleep if I touched another bitch."

"We did it to protect her. We had a brother who was a crazy fuck and the only way we could protect her was to put space between us," Razer answered.

"Yeah, was the hand that was playing with that girl's titty imaginary? Any one of these fucks do that to one of my bitches, I'm gonna cut his hand off." Killyama believed in giving fair warning. She leaned back in her seat when the Destructors lost their admiring expressions.

Evie tried to make up some lost ground. She was losing to these biker bitches and she was getting more and more pissed off.

"No, it wasn't imaginary. Razer had to prove she meant

nothing to him. Memphis had already tried to kill her twice. We had to make him believe he was in the clear after Bedford was arrested or he would never have made a clear move against us. We had to have proof he betrayed the club. We couldn't take someone outside the club's word as proof without evidence," Evie explained in front of everyone. Talking club business in front of others was breaking a rule, but they owed Beth an explanation and she wouldn't give them the opportunity. Truthfully, Evie didn't really blame her, though.

"So instead, you betrayed Beth. She's not club, so she didn't matter," Killyama threw the explanation back in Evie's face.

"She matters." This time it was Razer who spoke.

"Not enough," Crazy Bitch answered. "But I have a question I need answered." Turning to Beth, she asked, "The one with all the tats, he do anything to hurt you? Because my fingers are dying to see how far down those tats go."

Shade just stood there, ignoring the woman while keeping his expression bland. Beth could have sworn she saw a trace of fleeting worry in his eyes, however.

Beth was unable to stop herself. "No, he is the best of the bunch. Never saw him laying a hand on the women. Never drunk, didn't see him at the parties. I have no problem with Shade." Beth gave him a saccharine smile. She had told him she would pay him back for stopping her from leaving the house that day. It had taken a while, but she had gotten her revenge.

The Last Riders' mouths dropped open to a man and woman. Even though they knew she was throwing Shade under the bus, they could tell she believed what she'd said.

Natasha couldn't prevent the laughter bubbling from her throat and the other women from the club started laughing, too. "Are you serious? He's the wor—" Her voice was cut of immediately.

"Shut-up," Shade said, promising retribution if one

woman spoke another word.

"Damn, you had to go and blow it, telling her to shut-up. Don't let him talk to you that way, bitch. Still, if you fuck as good as you look, I could always tape your mouth shut."

"You aren't going to be touching nothing of his, bitch. Get on the back of my bike; we are leaving," a biker behind Ace yelled.

"I'm not going anywhere with you, Joker. We're going to Beth's house after we get done here. Sex Piston is going to cut her hair."

"No, she's not," Razer and Beth spoke at the same time.

Throwing a dirty look at Razer, she reminded her friends. "I was going to make an appointment next week, remember?"

"I'm going to save you the trip," Sex Piston said, slamming her drink down on the table, which caused what little was left to slosh over the side of the glass.

"She's going home with me. You're not touching her hair," Razer warned.

"I'm not going home with you," Beth argued.

"Yes, you are," Razer said between gritted teeth.

"No, I am not."

"Beth is not going anywhere with you." Crazy Bitch put her arm across the back of Beth's chair while the rest of the biker bitches also scooted their chairs closer to Beth.

"Back off," Evie cautioned.

"Listen to the bitch," Crazy Bitch taunted the men.

"I was talking to you," Evie said, stepping closer to the woman who was practically sitting on Beth's lap.

"Evie." Natasha tried to pull Evie back.

"Who are you?" Sex Piston asked.

"Natasha."

"What kind of name is that?"

"I haven't really been given a nickname yet."

"You the new member Viper fucked a couple of weeks ago and you let Beth think it was Razer?"

Natasha flushed, letting Evie's arm go.

"Viper didn't want anyone to know he was in town."

"Instead, it was easier to stick a knife in Beth's back. I can think of several names for you, but first there is something I wanna know, been wondering ever since they walked in the door. He fuck as good as he looks?" She pointed to Viper.

Natasha laughed. "Better."

"Damn."

"It don't matter how he fucks; none of you bitches are going to find out. Hell, he's keeping his own clubhouse of pussy warm, he's not getting mine. Now get on the fucking bikes!" Ace's face turned a mottled red.

It was The Last Riders looking at the other club in sympathy as the women just sat at the table ignoring the men that finally pushed Ace over the edge. "That's it." Ace moved forward to grab Sex Piston, who threw her glass at him. When he dodged it, he accidently shoved Knox who shoved back. Taking it as an aggressive move, one of Ace's men punched Knox. From there, complete and utter pandemonium ensued. Beth sat at the table in astonishment as the two clubs began fighting, taking their frustration with the women out on each other. Beth was almost thrown out of her chair when Evie ripped Crazy Bitch's arm off of her and the two women began fighting. Beth jumped up from the table when Sex Piston grabbed Natasha by the hair and slammed her face on the table.

"Which of these bitches is Bliss? I'm going to take care of her tonight, too," Sex Piston asked.

"Uh. I don't think she's here," Beth answered, searching through the crowd.

"Lucky bitch. I'll have to deal with her later then." Beth watched helplessly as she lifted Natasha by her hair and face slammed her again.

"Sex Piston, I think you're hurting her." Beth finally

made an attempt to stop her.

"Leave her alone, Beth. Let us deal with this," T.A. said with Jewell in a stranglehold.

"Stop. I don't want them hurt." The bar was now engulfed in fighting between both sexes. Bodies were flying, furniture was being broken, and the screams were as loud as the blaring music.

"Shit, we ain't going to hurt them much. We're just gonna teach them not to mess with you or they're gonna deal with us," T.A. replied, shaking a stunned Jewell. "What did she do?"

"Uh… nothing?" Beth couldn't think with all the bodies flying around the bar.

Before Beth could say another word, Razer had her by the waist and was throwing her over his shoulder as the Last Riders made a path for him to the door by simply throwing the Destructors out of the way.

"Put me down."

"Bring her back," Killyama screamed over the loud brawling.

Beth was barely able to lift herself up, though when she finally managed to get one more glimpse, the last thing she saw was the bar completely destroyed. Evie had gained the upper hand over Crazy Bitch and had her down on the floor on her stomach while sitting on her back, pulling the woman's arms backward. At the same time, Natasha lifted a vase that was on the table and used it to bash Sex Piston into releasing her.

Outside, Razer saw the car where Evie had parked it in a hurry. It was blocking the bikes. He was aware that she knew never to do that, so she must have been worried about Beth to make such a stupid mistake, however it was also rather fortuitous because Beth's small hands beating on his back had brought him the understanding that he wasn't going to be able to ride on his bike with her struggling. Opening the driver's door, he shoved her across the seat and got in behind the driver's wheel. Seeing that Evie had been smart enough to leave the keys in the ignition, he started the car and began to pull out of the lot just as the sheriff's and two deputy's cars were pulling in.

"Let me out!" Beth yelled.

"Sit back. I'm taking you home."

Beth sat back in a huff. Crossing her arms over her chest, she sat there in disdainful silence right up to the point where Razer passed her turnoff and was obviously headed to his house.

"Obviously you passed my house. Stop and let me out. I can walk home."

"You are not going to your house. That crazy bitch is not going near your hair."

"Crazy Bitch wasn't going to cut my hair. Sex Piston was; she's a hair stylist."

"One of those bitches is actually named Crazy Bitch?"

"Yes."

"Which one was she?"

"The one sitting next to me with her arm around my shoulders."

"Figures."

"What does that mean?"

"It means that I know how she got her nickname. Why in the fuck would you want to hang with women named Crazy Bitch and Sex Piston?"

"Oh, I don't know, probably the same reason I let a guy named Razer fuck me over," Beth said sarcastically.

"I didn't fuck you over. I protected you. We decided that it was the best way to keep you safe."

"We?"

"The eight original members. They set the rules for the club."

"I see, the club decided that I needed protection from Memphis and that you fucking Bliss would send that message. Well, I guess Memphis believed it since I am sitting safe and sound in this car. Mission accomplished. Job well done. Why is it safe to tell me now?"

"Memphis made his move. He tried to blow the factory and the house up. That gave us all the proof we needed."

"He tried to kill everyone?"

"Yes."

"But why?"

"The insurance money."

"Well, I'm glad you guys were able to stop him before anyone else was hurt. I'll have to tell the sheriff not to forget that I want to press charges on him for tampering with my brakes and hurting Lily."

"We didn't turn him in to the sheriff. The club handled it."

Beth swallowed as Razer pulled into the driveway of the house and smoothly parked the car in its normal spot. She didn't want to know how the club handled Memphis's betrayal. Getting out of the car, he opened the passenger door and reached inside. He took Beth's arm, trying to pull her resisting body out of the car.

"I am not going to go inside that house ever again. Take me home." She slapped at his restraining hold and found herself effortlessly pulled from the car and her stomach once again on his shoulder.

Ignoring her demands, Razer packed her inside the house and up the flight of steps to his room. Inside, he flipped on the light switch before dropping Beth onto the soft mattress.

Beth tried to scoot off, but found her ankle in his firm hold, pulling her toward him as he stood next to the bed. Her ankle was released only for her legs to be lifted to his shoulders, her pussy plastered to the front of his jeans. The hard length of him encased behind his jeans had her panties dampening, her body not listening to the recriminations her mind was demanding to dampen her building desire.

"Stop wiggling or I am not going to be able to wait."

"I am not doing this, Razer."

Beth's frantic movements increased and she felt her

legs lowered and wrapped around his waist as he leaned forward, covering her body. He paused long enough to remove his shirt before his lips gently covered hers. Thrown off guard, Beth's struggles slowed as Razer explored her mouth as if he had never kissed her before. Her lips unconsciously widened under his subtle guidance. His tongue seared the warm recesses of her mouth, creating warmth that was beginning to melt the ice she had encased herself in since she had seen him holding Bliss.

At the remembrance, Beth's struggles found new life and she tore her lips from his. Razer didn't accept defeat, though. Tracing her jawline with the tip of his tongue, he nuzzled into her neck with nibbling kisses and, when that didn't work, he sucked a small bit of flesh in his mouth to leave a faint mark.

A tear slid down her check to drop into the curve of her neck and Razer raised his head to see her crying. He could feel the torn response she was trying not to give him.

He leaned back, sitting on his knees beside the bed, and then pulled Beth into an upright position so her legs were on each side of his lean body. Carefully, his hand went to the bottom of her dress, which had been pooled around her waist from her struggles. Pulling it upwards, he took it off her body. Beth sat before him in a lacy black bra and tiny, matching panties.

Her hands lifted to grab her dress, but Razer tossed it to the floor. "I am not going to fuck you, Razer. You can't make me," she said defiantly.

Razer hid his smile, noting her nipples were hard nubs clearly visible through her thin bra and, even through the dark material of her panties, he could see she was wet for him. Nevertheless, Razer didn't want to hurt her pride. He had done that for the last time. It was time for his pride to take the hit and he didn't try to make it easy on himself.

He took her hands, straightening her arms and twisting them to where he could see the marks on both sides.

Nausea drowned out the desire in his balls. Counting carefully, he counted the tiny scars on her arms; six sets of punctures wounds.

"Kitten," he said through a thickened voice.

"Razer?" Ignoring her, he stood up and pulled her up before him, turning her around. He smoothly undid her bra while ignoring her grabbing it and holding it to cover her breasts. Feeling ashamed, he lowered his head and kissed the faded, silvery scars that traced her back intermittently. How he had never noticed before he didn't know. When he turned her back to facing him, he gently pushed her back down into a sitting position on the side of the bed.

Not trying to take away the loosened bra, Razer searched her body thoroughly. He was about to stop, thinking he had found all the scars her sick bastard of a father had inflicted on her, when a thought struck him. He lifted her feet and at first seeing nothing except smooth flesh, he started to place them back on the floor, yet the rough texture stopped him. When he lifted them, Beth fell back on the bed, bracing herself on her elbows.

"Sweet, sweet, kitten." Razer blinked back the unmanly tears that pooled in his eyes. The bottoms of her feet were a mess. There were so many scars that there was no beginning and no end. They blended into each other and made the hours of torture she had withstood plainly visible on the flesh of her feet.

"What did he make you stand on?"

"Razer?"

"What did he make you stand on?" he ground out through gritted teeth.

Beth sighed. "Nails. He said God bore the pain for the sins of mankind. I could bear it for the sins I had committed."

"If he wasn't dead, God as my witness, I would kill him."

"It was a long time ago. Did Cash tell you? He knew

about the bites and the strap, but he shouldn't have known about the nails. No one knew. He only started doing that after the Sheriff threatened him. He'd even bragged at how the Sheriff wouldn't think to look there."

"Why didn't you go to the Sheriff and tell him. You went to him when your father beat Lily. Why not when he started doing this?"

"Because he didn't do this to Lily. I told him I would tell, so he left Lily alone other than being overly strict."

"Why not stop him from hurting you, not just Lily?"

"Because they would have taken us away from my parents. I couldn't do that to Lily. She loved them. They gave her what she had never had before and I couldn't lose my sister. I loved her, Razer, from the minute they brought her home, and I would do anything for her."

"I know, kitten." He pulled her into his arms, holding her close. His hand sliding through her silky hair until she was staring into his eyes.

"Did you forgive him?"

"I don't want to talk about him anymore." Beth tried to turn her head, but he held her immobile.

"Answer me. Did you forgive him?" Razer already knew the answer. Beth's loving heart was incapable of holding a grudge; the marks on her body proved that. It was that hope he had to hold onto.

"Yes, I forgave him, but that doesn't mean I am a doormat and going to forgive you." Beth started struggling against him again, trying to get away from the hard body holding her close. "You lied to me. You made me believe you wouldn't touch another woman without telling me and breaking it off with me first. Instead, you made Bliss come right in front of my face." It took all of Razer's strength to hold her down.

"I didn't lie to you. I did not fuck Bliss that night or any of the other girls since the day I had lunch with you at the diner. I touched Bliss that day, but I did it to put on a show for Memphis and to drive you away. She came, but I

205

wasn't even hard. I was too sick at the look on your face. I won't lie, either, just to make you feel better. Bliss wasn't the only one I touched to sidetrack Memphis, but I didn't fuck them. I wasn't even tempted to."

Beth didn't believe him. He had taken Bliss to his room that night and Razer had told her himself that he never turned away pussy. She also knew, without a doubt in her mind, that Bliss would have used every skill at her disposal to tempt him once in his room.

"I can see you don't believe me, but I am telling you the truth. I guess I'm going have to prove it to you. I can be faithful to you from now on and I will. These last few weeks were hell on me, waiting for Memphis to make his move and knowing how bad I hurt you in the process."

"It's not only the women I don't trust you with, Razer. You let the club decide what was best for us. You should have told me and I could have at least been prepared, but you threw me away instead."

"No, kitten, I never threw you away. I thought it was the best way because your reaction made it believable. Viper and the club waited three years for revenge, I couldn't take that away from them; he was my brother, too."

Beth understood. He had been torn between the club he loved and a woman he hadn't been with long. What had convinced her were not his words, but his face. Razer was always kind of a goof, joking around, never taking anything serious. Now, there was something different about him; a sorrow in his eyes, though there was also a resolve when he looked at her that had not been there before. Beth knew they had a long journey ahead of them, but it was a journey she had to take.

Razer could see understanding beginning to show in her features, although it did not take away the hurt still in her eyes. Razer knew it was going to take time to heal the pain he had intentionally inflicted and he was cool with that. Dean had been right all along, she was worth the wait.

He pulled at the bra Beth still had grasped tightly in her hand, throwing it and not caring where it landed. His lips covered one coral tipped breast while his fingers twisted the nipple on the other one. When she finally began to twist underneath him to get closer, he let go of the now shiny, hard nub.

"Now I am going to fuck you for what is left of the night. When we wake up in the morning and, after I fuck you again, I'll borrow the car so we can drive to your house and you can pack your bags to move your ass back in my room."

When Beth would have argued again, his lips went back to her nipple and this time his other hand stroked her silken pussy. After several minutes, when he felt she was close to coming, he again stopped, leaving her hanging.

"I can't live in your home. I would be too caged in. And it won't work between us, you living there and me here. You would begin having doubts about me when I am here and you're there. Even though I'm telling you that I'm not going to be touching or letting the women touch me anymore because I know that's what you want."

"I can't Razer. What about Lily?"

"The weekends Lily comes home and the vacations, even the summer one, I'll move in with you," Razer conceded.

"You will?"

"Yes, but Fridays during the long vacation, we are here. We can go home afterward, but we come for the party. I'll need to relax after being nice all week."

"That works for me." Beth smiled.

"We're going to take the best from both of our worlds and make one of our own."

This time, when Razer sucked her nipple into his mouth, he bit down and thrust his fingers deep within her wet pussy. Beth arched into his mouth; the small bite of pain at her breast had wetness lubricating his fingers, allowing him to plunge another digit deep within her. Razer moved to his side, continuing to play with her body until her heels were planted firmly on the mattress and she was thrusting her hips were. When her body arched and forced her breasts upward, he leaned forward and took a nipple in his mouth once again.

Beth's hands went to Razer's shoulders and the smooth flesh heightened her desire. She loved touching him; sometimes just a simple touch of his hand against hers made Beth want him. She was not going to say no to him, she couldn't. Her father had tortured and abused her during her childhood—tortures that she and Lily would never tell—but nothing had hurt her as badly as being without Razer. Her searching hands discovered that he had also lost weight. She was definitely not the only one who had suffered from their absence of each other.

Beth moaned as Razer slid down her body, kissing her along the way. When he reached her belly button, he played with the tiny, glinting diamond. "This is sexy as hell, kitten. It makes my cock hard when I see it through your clothes. It tells me how naughty you are."

Beth's hand shifted through his soft hair as his lips slid down further, his hands pulling down her panties to leave her naked to his gaze. Beth blushed, aware of what he was staring at.

"It itches when it grows back in. It was easier to shave it—" Beth tried to explain, however Razer cut her off.

"Kitten." Razer kissed her bare mound while a part of him eased. Razer took it for what it was; Beth had never given up hope that they would get back together, no matter how angry she had been.

No one had ever cared enough to miss him. Raised in foster homes, he had entered the military when he had graduated high school. Razer had never had a family at all until he had joined The Last Riders. The women who had come and gone in his life had always only wanted one thing from him; the sex he had become accomplished at performing. He had used his body to take and give pleasure, but he had never given himself away emotionally.

From the first moment he had seen Beth, something had come to life inside of him and never having had it before, he hadn't known what it was. It was love. Like a child learning, he had taken it for granted; used it, smashed it, then almost destroyed it. The fledgling emotion that had come alive in him, though, was like Beth; strong and resilient.

Razer was in love with Beth. He had finally admitted it to himself the day they had visited Lily at her college. When she had gone inside the station and those biker bitches had followed her, he had almost lost his mind. He had been following her inside when the bikers had challenged him. Thankfully, it was quickly handled with Shade there; the other bikers being inept against two former Navy Seals. Beth had returned minutes later, oblivious to what had transpired during her absence.

Beth's body twisted underneath him as his mouth found her pussy. He separated the flesh, finding the tiny button and sucked it into his mouth. Razer teased the bundle of nerves with small bites and lavish attention while Beth's legs spread further, giving him greater access. A finger found the wetness and he pushed it deep into her warm channel. Razer used every skill at his disposal to have her tensing, ready to explode.

"My kitty wants to come?" Razer asked, delving another finger inside her.

"Yes… Yes…" Beth moaned. Her hips surged upwards, trying to maneuver his fingers to the right spot so that she could come.

"Not yet… we're going to play for a while." Razer played with her body, tormenting her until she was covered with a sheen of sweat and her frustrated whimpers were driving him crazy. Still, he denied her the climax. When she tore away from him, unable to take more, he dragged her back.

"You sure you want me, kitten?"

"Yes." Razer's mouth latched onto her as he heard her answer. This time when his tongue found her clit, he gave it the pressure needed for her to finally come. Beth almost lost consciousness, the relief was so great. Afterward, Beth lay limp on the bed with Razer leaning over her, his hand rubbing her stomach while he enjoyed watching her recover.

"Jerk." Razer grinned in accomplishment at her word.

"Do you really want to insult me?" He lifted a brow as his fingers returned to her moist pussy.

"No, I don't." Beth was no fool, but she did believe in revenge.

She rose to her knees with a mischievous grin. Unsnapping his jeans, she tugged them down as he lay back with his arms folded behind his head. After tugging the jeans free, she shoved them off the bed and turned back to Razer and stared. Crawling to his side, she sat on her knees, unable to believe her eyes. Her eyes furiously blinked back the tears threatening to break loose.

"You put my name on your dick."

"Not quite, but as close as it was going to get."

Beth stared down in awe at the tattoo slightly above his hardened cock. It was a horizontal, purple ribbon with her name on it, in what resembled her own handwriting.

"I took a piece of paperwork that you left behind with your signature. The tattoo artist used it as a pattern. I rode two states away to have it done."

"Did you pass out?"

"No, but it was close." Beth couldn't help laughing. She had never seen Razer embarrassed.

"How close?"

"I threw up."

Beth's eyes searched his, seeing what he was trying to tell her. Her finger traced the tattoo. "It's beautiful." Her lips lowered, tracing the tattoo with her tongue. "When did you get it?"

"While you were in the hospital. I couldn't stay in Treepoint while you were in there and not be with you. Since I had to leave, I got the tattoo while I was away. I only got back a couple of hours before you got released."

Razer's hand went to her hair and used it to raise her head. "Evie was going to bring you the suitcase and tell you to stay away. We thought that would be the best way to break it off, but you came to the club and we had to play it out in front of Memphis. I'm sorry, kitten."

"I don't want to talk about it anymore. Okay?"

"Okay." Razer knew that it was going to take time for that hurt to heal; she felt as if everyone had betrayed her. In a way, they had. They had put Memphis ahead of Beth because he had been a member and Beth wasn't. It was going to have to be resolved. Razer loved his brothers and Beth. He needed them both. There was only one way for that to happen, Beth had to become a member.

Beth's mouth sucked his cock into her warm mouth, her tongue tracing the length of him before exploring the head of his cock, finding the sensitive nerves underneath. Razer's hips surged upwards, trying get her to take more of him inside her mouth. Instead, she pulled off him completely, blowing soft breaths on him and then giving him an innocent smile. Razer's eyes narrowed, he had forgotten one thing while he had played with her mercilessly, that she was a firm believer in revenge.

Beth's fingers found his balls, exploring his body, something she had been too shy to do before. When she eventually sucked one of his balls into her mouth, Razer almost came off the bed in surprise. Beth showed him that she was the master at playing. This time it was him covered in sweat before she took his cock deep inside her tight throat, setting a rhythm that had him grasping her head as he thrust wildly out of control with the pleasure tightening his balls until he came with a loud groan.

As Beth leaned back on her knees, Razer could only stare at her in amazement while trying to catch his breath.

She was going to be a good match for him. He hadn't thought of it before; however, the best part of sex—the part he always enjoyed—was the playing and cats loved to play.

CHAPTER TWENTY-TWO

Razer and Beth went down to breakfast late. They were at the bottom of the steps before the unusual quietness and lack of the aromas coming from the kitchen struck them. By this time of day, someone should be in the kitchen cooking lunch. Giving each other worried looks, they went into the kitchen, coming to a sudden stop.

Everyone was in the huge kitchen and attached dining room. All the available space was occupied by a member in various states of injuries. Evie was sitting on the stool with her hands in a bowl of ice, Jewell was holding an ice pack to the back of her neck, Natasha held a bag of frozen vegetables to the side of her swollen face while Ember and Dawn—who Beth hadn't been aware were even at the bar—were dabbing alcohol on various scratches and that was just the women.

The men were in even worse shape. Viper and Shade seemed to have been injured the worst; their shirts were off and both sets of ribs were taped. Their faces were battered with split lips. Viper had a piece of medical tape across a swollen nose and Shade had a black eye. Each were holding frozen steaks against their faces. Beth's gaze swept the room. The other members hadn't fared much better. Cash, Rider and Knox seemed to have the least of the injuries with busted knuckles, split lips and bruised faces. Each of them was holding frozen vegetables to their heads. Train, who had two black eyes, was holding another steak to his face. Bliss, the only one uninjured, was passing around beer and ibuprofen.

All eyes turned to them as Beth and Razer surveyed the damage.

"I think we better order some pizza," Beth told Razer, seeing all the food in use.

"Did the Destructors look as bad?" Razer asked.

"The men did," Viper said, taking a beer from Bliss.

"The women?" Beth asked hesitantly, twisting her hands together.

"We don't know. They were sitting at the bar drinking when the Sheriff and his men arrested us," Shade said, glaring at Beth.

"You were taken to jail?" Razer asked in surprise, staring at Viper.

"We all were. Held us until bond was posted an hour ago. Tried to call you, but you weren't answering," Shade stated through gritted teeth.

"Figured you were kind of busy," Evie said with a hesitant smile.

"Where was Bliss?"

"We didn't call her. Beth's new bff's were waiting outside the Sheriff's office to jump her," Shade said in a voice promising retribution.

"Sheriff thought it would be better for everyone's safety if she stayed here," Viper cut in.

"She could have relayed the message to me." Razer didn't even know where his phone was currently. Probably buried in the pile of clothes on the floor of his room.

"They wanted you, too. Those bitches weren't very happy with the way you packed Beth out of the Pink Slipper."

"Why didn't the Sheriff just arrest them?"

214

"He did. He put us in one and the Destructors in the other."

"So who posted bail?"

"An impartial party."

"An impartial party? Who?"

"Pastor Dean. The Sheriff figured they wouldn't attack a man of the cloth." Shade took another beer from Bliss with a shaking hand. "The crazy one asked for his number."

"Crazy Bitch?" Beth asked, pleased.

The bottle Shade was lifting to his busted mouth froze. "That her name?"

"Yes." Beth nodded.

"And you made frien—"

Razer cut him off. "Don't go there, you won't like the answer."

Shade took a long drink of his beer before putting the bottle down carefully on the counter with a still shaking hand. All eyes were on him, tensely waiting, except Beth, who was handing Train a paper towel to wipe the blood away from his dripping nose.

"I am going to bed."

Beth nodded. "I'm sure you'll feel much better after getting some sleep."

Shade's lips tightened into a thin line. Limping slowly to the doorway, he stopped by Beth, who looked up from holding pressure to Train's nose. Razer, Cash and Knox shifted unobtrusively closer to Beth.

"Is your sister like you?" Shade asked.

Confused by his question, Beth answered honestly, "No, we're the complete opposite of each other."

"Good." He continued to the doorway.

"Everyone always assumed I was the troublemaker, but I was the one always having to get Lily out of some trouble she managed to get herself involved in before she went to college. Actually, her being away is giving me a break. Of course I would never admit that to her."

215

Shade's shoulders slumped. Stopping by the counter full of liquor bottles that were used to restock the bar, he grabbed a bottle of whiskey before leaving.

Beth went to Evie, checking on her bruised knuckles. "I hope it doesn't hurt too bad." She handed her a dish towel that she took out of a drawer.

Ruefully, Evie took the towel, wrapping some ice in it to hold in her hand. "In comparison to how much you were hurt, I deserved what happened. Those women stood up for you when we didn't. I am truly sorry for how we treated you, we all are. It was because of you that we were able to prove who killed Gavin. Memphis betrayed the club while you were going to let Bedford shoot you to protect it."

"We decided the best way to pay you back was to make you a member," Viper broke into the women's conversation.

Beth immediately shook her head. "Thanks, but I am not going to have sex to get the votes."

"You already have the votes. All eight. First time it has happened in the club's history."

"How?"

"Well," Viper said wickedly, "Some of the votes you earned the usual way; Knox, Rider and Razer. I gave you my marker at the hospital when Lily was hurt, which I decided would be my vote. Cash and Train gave you their marker because they were in the service with Gavin." Viper took a minute before continuing, "Because of you, we were able to recover his body and give him a proper burial. The last two members expect repayment at their discretion from Razer. Which I believe he will agree to." Razer nodded, relieved that the club had acknowledged the importance of Beth both to him and The Last Riders.

"Let's go get your tat," Natasha said, her smile bright, eagerly wanting to resume their friendship.

Beth shook her head. "Not today, I want you girls to go, and I don't think some of you are up to it." Turning to

Razer, "Can you go? I know you're not anxious to go to a tattoo shop after you just got a new one, but would you mind?"

"You got a new tat? Why didn't you show us? Where is it at? Your back? Let us see," Bliss said.

Beth saw the expectant faces in the room. "No one has seen the tattoo?"

The members not understanding, shook their heads as Beth began to cry at the overwhelming sense of relief from knowing that Razer had truly not been with anyone since her.

"Why not? You get a pussy tattoo?" Rider asked in disbelief. Razer turned bright red, taking a crying Beth in his arms.

"Rider, I can guarantee you will never know," Razer promised.

CHAPTER TWENTY-THREE

Penni heard the distinctive notes of her cell phone ringing as she lay on her bed reading a book. The caller ID brought a smile to her lips. With a swipe of her finger, she answered.

"Hey bro, what's up?"

"Why does anything have to be up for me to call? Can't I call and check on my little sister?"

A snort sounded clearly through the line.

"How is school?"

"Good, would have been better if Mom and Dad would actually let me go without having to live at home." Penni hadn't been able to come up with a valid argument for leaving home when they lived within a few miles of the University of Ohio.

"I could help convince them to let you go to an out of state college."

"What's the catch?" Suspicion laced her voice.

"It has to be the college of my choice."

"What's the name of the college?" Penni was almost bouncing in excitement.

"Breckinridge College."

"Don't recognize the name. Let me check it out on the

web. Hang on."

Before he could protest, the phone was set down. It didn't take long before she came back on the line. "No, thanks." All excitement was gone from her voice.

"Come on, give it a chance."

"No."

His snort could be heard over the line this time. "What will it take?"

"A car, a generous allowance and a vacation of my choice every summer."

"Okay. Do the paperwork. I'll talk to the parents."

"That's not all." She wasn't finished.

"Penni..." he warned.

"A reason?"

Several minutes of silence met her question.

"Someone needs a friend."

That she could do. "Deal."

* * *

Shade hung up the phone as Beth and Lily approached the picnic table he was sitting at, waiting for everyone to return from the buffet.

"Where's Razer?" Beth asked.

"Getting the drinks."

The two women sat down on one side of the table with filled plates. The church picnic was filled with the congregation and The Last Riders celebrating the Fourth of July. It was a beautiful day with everyone laughing and having fun. Everyone except Lily, who had spent the last hour trying unsuccessfully to convince her sister to let her switch colleges.

Razer set drinks down in front of everyone before sitting down next to Beth, who promptly gave him her shoulder.

"How long you going to stay mad?" he asked, picking up his hamburger.

"At least past that date you had tatted on your razor knife."

219

"Still can't understand why you're so mad. I thought it would make you happy," Razer said in his own defense.

"Most women get engaged with a romantic dinner and a ring, not the guy pointing to a tattoo then saying 'let's do it'."

"No sense in putting it off with a bun in the oven," Razer shrugged.

Beth choked on her hamburger. "I am not pregnant," she said to Lily who was laughing at the couple's argument.

"You will be if we miss that date," Razer threatened. "Take a drink before you choke to death."

Beth angrily lifted the paper cup to her lips, staring in bemusement at the diamond glinting at her from the bottom of the empty cup.

Beth shakily reached inside, pulling out the beautiful ring.

Razer took it from her, sliding it on her finger and then giving her a tender kiss.

"Is this romantic enough?" he asked, brushing the tear off her cheek with his thumb.

"It's perfect."

Also by Jamie Begley

The Last Riders Series:

Razer's Ride

Viper's Run

The VIP Room Series:

Teased

The Dark Souls Series:

Soul Of A Man

ABOUT THE AUTHOR

"I was born in a small town in Kentucky. My family began poor, but worked their way to owning a restaurant. My mother was one of the best cooks I have ever known, and she instilled in all her children the value of hard work, and education.

Taking after my mother, I've always love to cook, and became pretty good if I do say so myself. I love to experiment and my unfortunate family has suffered through many. They now have learned to steer clear of those dishes. I absolutely love the holidays and my family put up with my zany decorations.

For now, my days are spent at work and I write during the nights and weekends. I have two children who both graduate next year from college. My daughter does my book covers, and my son just tries not to blush when someone asks him about my books.

Currently I am writing three series of books- The Last Riders that is fairly popular, The Dark Souls series, which is not, and The VIP Room, which we will soon see. My favorite book I have written is Soul Of A Woman, which I am hoping to release during the summer of 2014. It took me two years to write, during which I lost my mother, and brother. It's a book that I truly feel captures the true depths of love a woman can hold for a man. In case you haven't figured it out yet, I am an emotional writer who wants the readers to feel the emotion of the characters they are reading. Because of this, Teased is probably the hardest thing I have written.

All my books are written for one purpose- the enjoyment others find in them, and the expectations of my fans that inspire me to give it my best. In the near future I hope to take a weekend break and visit Vegas that will hopefully be next summer. Right now I am typing away on Knox's story and looking forward to the coming holidays. Did I mention I love the holidays?"

Jamie loves receiving emails from her fans,
JamieBegley@ymail.com

Find Jamie here,
https://www.facebook.com/AuthorJamieBegley

Get the latest scoop at Jamie's official website,
JamieBegley.net

Printed in Poland
by Amazon Fulfillment
Poland Sp. z o.o., Wrocław